In the bedroom she removed her garter belt and stockings. Switching on the soft lights, she walked to the mirror and stared at herself; at every delightful feminine curve; at the full breasts, the long, tapering thighs. There was only one reason why Martha didn't despise the sight completely. She hated being a woman. She hated being so damned curvaceous. She hated the fact that even her severely tailored suits and closely cropped hairdo couldn't make her look like a man.

There was only one reason, she thought, why I can tolerate this womanly facade I carry around. At least, being attractive myself, I can attract the beautiful women I want to possess.

ALL THE GAY GIRLS

By Margurite Frame

A Gold Star Original Novel

A GOLD STAR BOOK

Published by The New International Library, Inc.

Chapter I

ALTHOUGH VERONICA had wakened early, it was close to eleven o'clock before she made her appearance downstairs. She had spent the intervening hours tossing and turning restlessly in her elaborate bed; dozing off from time to time in a determined but doomed effort to stop thinking; waking from time to time to glance at the clock and fall back into her unhappy reverie.

It was Thursday, and exactly one month from the morning in which she'd first discovered that her second marriage was racing toward its own destruction at an alarming pace. She'd spent the intervening weeks in what even she had to realize as an emotional vacuum from which she peered forth at the world.

Kirk, the husband with whom she had thought herself so desperately in love, had spent those same weeks trying to discover exactly what was going on in the mind of his lovely, and suddenly inaccessible wife. Needless to say, he had failed. Veronica had always been close-mouthed about her thoughts, and this heart-breaking discovery of her dissatisfaction with Kirk was kept a deep secret from everyone, including Kirk himself.

As she began to dress for her luncheon appointment she mulled over his probable reaction to the decision she'd finally reached—not, as she'd first planned, to divorce him—but to find herself some kind of interesting work in one last attempt to save her marriage by keeping herself too busy to dwell on her own unhappiness. As she brushed the golden tips of her short, auburn hair she wondered what part of her inner make-up was missing. Why, she thought, am I so incapable of holding on to my love for any one man? From her first short, shining college romance through her first short and not quite so shining marriage and the intervening romances before Kirk, she had found herself wholly unable to continue giving herself to her lovers with the original delight and satisfaction. Always, after a few incredibly lovely months, Veronica would leave them, her farewell gift the spurious fragments of what once had been.

Men, she pondered, can't *all* be wrong. There has to be something the matter with me. I wonder if I should try a psychiatrist instead of a job? We can certainly afford it. She smoothed the last, almost invisible wrinkle from her sheer nylons as she shook her head. "No," she spoke aloud, "I'd rather do it myself."

Veronica walked down the graceful stairway (for which she'd *had* to have this house and no other), out across the well tended terrace and getting into her white T-Bird roared down the driveway, ready for battle.

She hadn't, it suddenly occurred to her, even spoken to her husband this morning.

Martha Browning (known to her more intimate friends as "Marty"), the highly polished and highly paid vice-president of one of the most expensive cosmetic companies on the West Coast, was having what she referred to as "a bitch of a morning." When she'd arrived at the luxurious offices situated in one of the new all-glass buildings on Sunset Strip, Martha had been in one of her better moods. Things had been going smoothly at work, and the luncheon appointment she had with the wealthy and beautiful Veronica Wade, for the purpose of adding her to the already long list of attractive women beneath her "motherly" wing, had been a source of pleasurable imaginings for days.

The mood had quickly dissipated as Martha walked past the sullen blonde receptionist who stared knowingly, and with a great deal of resentment, as she noticed both Martha's mood and the unusually tailored suit and blouse she was wearing.

Damn, thought Martha angrily, I should never have mixed business and pleasure with *that* one! She's done nothing but bug me for "seconds" ever since. If, she added determinedly, she doesn't wise up and stop being so obvious, I'm going to have to get rid of her, and that could be messy—or, more to the point, quite expensive.

Martha entered her office without even nodding at the receptionist and closed the door firmly behind her. Before she reached her desk the buzz of the intercom sounded. The cold, blonde voice announced that New York was calling. Twenty minutes later, Martha hung up and angrily summoned the chief and three of her assistants from the art department.

"New York," she informed them cuttingly, "is *not* delighted with the layouts for the new 'Movie Starlet' campaign." She stood up, moving from behind her desk to the center of the room, then whirling to face the four unhappy artists. "Not only is New York not 'delighted'—they think it stinks!"

"But, Miss Browning—"

"But me no 'buts,' " Martha interrupted before the words of the artist had fully left her lips. "I want a new layout as early as possible. I want a new layout before *this* day is over. And," she added, the sarcasm dripping like molasses from her quiet words, "I want a layout with—and I quote directly from New York—'Taste, integrity and appeal to someone other than the untrained, unskilled, part-time working women of America.' "

"But, Miss Browning—"

7

Martha's voice was vitriolic as she once again broke in on the artist. "Before *this* day is over, I think I said. And that, Miss Sarak, leaves no time for conversation!"

The artist nodded meekly, and the four thoroughly cowed women left the office. Martha wasn't the least bit curious as to what her artist had been trying to say. She knew only too well.

The entire "Movie Starlet" campaign had been Martha's idea—from conception to completion. There had even been, as Martha recalled, several objections from the art department as to the theme and copy submitted. She'd overridden all of them, sure of herself, and she thought bitterly, of her "taste, integrity, and appeal, etcetera!" Quite naturally, she hadn't mentioned this point to the angry New York office. And, quite naturally, when she'd refused to allow the artists to mention it in the sanctity of her private office, she knew they would not dare mention it elsewhere.

Martha controlled her employees with the iron hand method. And to gripe or complain about her treatment was almost the same as giving notice.

The intercom buzzed again. It was the blonde.

"May I have Edna relieve me a few minutes, *Miss* Browning? I'd like to see you—in private, if I may."

Martha sighed wearily, gazed for a moment out the wall of glass overlooking the city of Los Angeles, then nodding to herself replied, "If Edna is free now, I can spare a few minutes." She flicked the intercom off without awaiting a reply and picked up a handful of papers, intending to look as busy and distant as possible. No use, she thought, trying to dodge this issue any longer. I should have known better, but hell—she was new, she was attractive and she made it evident she was willing. How the devil was I to know it was a first-time thing with her and would send her completely off her track? Lord, she winced, the gal has a husband and two kids! If New York ever learns about this, I'm really sunk.

8

Her office door opened, and the blonde walked in filled with a mixture of fright and desperation. She closed the door behind her, walked across the room and leaning dramatically across Martha's desk said, "You've been avoiding me. Every possible way you've been avoiding me. After *that* night, how could you? How do you dare? You must remember what happened—what you said— what we did. After all that, how can you act like this to me?"

Martha stared at her in silence. Without any warning whatsoever, the blonde girl broke into wrenching sobs.

"I don't have the slightest idea what you're talking about," Martha said, ignoring the girl's tears. "But I do know one thing. When you take up my good time—in my office—it had better be about business. About business, and nothing else. Do you understand?"

"But—you—" and the blonde dissolved once again into tears.

It was then that Martha realized she was really having one bitch of a morning. And it was then that Martha decided the time had come to bring the entire mess to a screaming halt. The fact that she'd been the protagonist bothered her not at all. After considering her part, she still had several facts on her side. She hadn't forced the girl. She hadn't knocked her down and made her go along with the action. She hadn't of course, she realized, been exactly thoughtful in her choice of partners; what was the word New York had used? Taste. She'd shown no taste at all. But the fact remained that the blonde had been more than willing. She wasn't angry about what *had* happened. She was angry because it *hadn't* happened again.

"I think," Martha spoke with venom in her voice, "you'd better give your notice. You seem to have confused a short, fast evening of fun—a quick trick—with a world-shattering love affair. You—"

"You can't fire me!" the blonde managed between her sniffles. "I'll tell everybody. I'll call New York—"

9

"Try it, baby," Martha snarled. "You just go ahead and try it. There are a few calls I can make too, and don't you forget it. If you don't care about your husband, that's one thing. But I don't think even *you*," and the word was laced with vicious threads of hatred, "would want the parents of your kids' friends, or the teachers at their schools, to know about their mother."

The blonde looked at Martha with bewildered horror.

"Shall we say two weeks pay—in lieu of notice? Now if you'll excuse me, I have a luncheon appointment." Martha stood up, sure of her safety, and grabbing her purse from the bookcase behind her desk, strode from the office. The blonde didn't come out for almost an hour. When she did she picked up her purse and walked out of the building.

She didn't even tell the long-suffering Edna that she wouldn't be back. Not that afternoon. Not ever.

Chapter II

VERONICA WAVED a slightly giddy good-by as Martha Browning hopped into the Yellow Cab and gave the driver a set of slurred instructions for her destination. Their luncheon meeting had been a long and completely successful one from the standpoint of getting to know each other (and getting a job for Veronica). Foodwise, it had been a different tale entirely; after Martha's fourth, crisply ordered, round of Martinis, Veronica had given up on the prospect of dining and given in to a liquid afternoon.

As the attendant pulled up in her T-Bird, she asked him to put the top down for her. Even though it was close to four-thirty, and the afternoon ocean breezes were beginning to cool the warm California air, Veronica realized she needed some sort of a sobering influence far more than she needed comfort.

What a bitch of an afternoon, she thought to herself, as she climbed behind the wheel and slowly pulled away from the canopied entrance of the smart restaurant. And what an odd, almost weird character, was this Martha (call me Marty away from the office, dear) Browning. Dianne should have warned me, she mused, as she recklessly swerved to pass a more civic-minded Continental driver. She did tell me her friend was rather "severe," which would be only natural for a woman fighting the field of male mastery which controlled the heights of business to which Martha had struggled. But Dianne didn't tell me, Veronica added to herself, through the cloud of Martinis, that Marty was a lesbian.

Veronica hadn't met too many lesbians during her young life, but the minute Martha had lit her first cigarette, and then patted her hand in a strangely uncomfortable, and uncomfortably thrilling manner, she'd known. As the realization hit her she recalled vaguely the rumors she'd heard about Dianne: her unenviable record of seven ex-husbands, and the whispered stories of amoral "switch-hitting." I guess, Veronica giggled through her gin-flavored haze, the stories were true. It's no wonder she's a set of nerves as taut as a piano wire.

What's the difference? she asked herself. The woman certainly wouldn't want such a thing known about the office, and I'm equally sure she must have her own circle of friends for that sort of thing. No matter—I am now the chief receptionist for the vice president of Amour Cosmetics. What was that horrible name Marty'd been bragging about? "Movie Starlet?" Veronica giggled again as she barely missed the fender of a small, bright yellow sports car. Through the mist which was beginning to fade from an alcoholic shimmer to a dull headache, her new position as one of the "working women" of the world still glimmered attractively.

No more divorces for this little girl, she reminded herself. And if Dianne has any idea I might go the other route, she can forget it. I may not dig Kirk anymore, but if I take a lover it's going to be another *man*. That's for sure!

As she turned the car into the driveway of her lovely home she began to think about her husband and the reaction she might get from him when she broke the news about her job. He'll be mad enough about that, she thought soberly. But if he knew I was working for a *les*,

12

he'd absolutely flip. She laughed out loud as she parked the car. "I couldn't care less."

Veronica walked slowly, concentrating on hiding any signs of tipsiness. As she entered the house, her thoughts were once again on Marty. I must, she remembered, start thinking of her as "Miss Browning."

She didn't, at first, hear Kirk's greeting.

Marty Browning had not returned to her office after her luncheon with Veronica, who she was already thinking of as "Ronnie." She'd directed the cabbie to her swank apartment building, and as she unlocked the door of her own suite realized she'd overtipped him by at least a buck. The afternoon had gone so perfectly though, that her usual resentment of parting with loot for any purpose other than making a new "trick" didn't faze her. Thank God Dianne set this one up for me, she thought as she kicked off her shoes and threw her tailored suit coat across the vivid red couch.

She was humming happily to herself as she went into the kitchen. She headed straight to the refrigerator and took out a bottle of ice-cold gin. Picking up a double-sized shot glass she poured herself a hefty drink and slugged it down without a chaser. What a sweet little pigeon this Ronnie would make, she whispered to herself. Pouring another drink, she took a short sip and walked back into the living room. Placing the drink carefully on the marble coffee table she removed her blouse and skirt, then her bra and slip, rubbing her hands over her full breasts in anticipatory pleasure.

Sweet Veronica Wade. How her husband is going to miss her!

Suddenly her mood changed. It was all well and good, she muttered angrily, to plan on making a new girl, but she was in need of some recreation *tonight*. And the sooner, the better. She hadn't, she realized, recognized how exciting the afternoon had been. She should have cut

13

it off earlier—before this need had become aroused. For a moment she regretted having kicked her most recent lover out when she found her cheating. But only for a moment. That bitch, she remembered. Cheating was bad enough, but not in the bed she'd been sharing with me.

Tossing off the second drink, she headed for the empty bedroom. Tonight, she promised herself, I'll find myself a one-time chick. That's all there is to it. But soon! She began to hum again in a mercurial change of temperament. "Soon—it's gonna be—Ronnie and me."

In the bedroom, she removed her garter belt and stockings. Switching on the soft lights she walked to the mirror and stared at herself; at every delightful feminine curve; at the full breasts, the long, tapering thighs. There was only one reason why Marty didn't despise the sight completely. She hated being a woman. She hated being so damned curvaceous. She hated the fact that even her severely tailored suits and closely cropped hair-do couldn't make her look like a man. She despised the men in the industry who took every opportunity they could find—and Marty made them difficult to locate—to make a pass at her. Some of them, she knew full well, were more interested in her position (and her income) than her body. Unfortunately, many of them put the body in first place.

There was only one reason, she thought, why I can tolerate this womanly facade I carry around. At least, being attractive myself, I can attract the beautiful women I want to possess. Women who might be repelled by one of the "lucky" dykes who looked like dykes—those kind I can usually get for myself.

Like, she added gratefully, like Ronnie Wade.

Marty showered, discarding plan after plan for her evening "cruise." Face it, baby, she finally told herself, you're not about to get to Ronnie yet. And if you can't have the cream of the crop tonight, get yourself decked

14

out in full drag and hit a place like "The Song"—you can always get some kind of action there, even if you have to pay for it.

Out of the shower, determination in every muscle of her female-male body, she began to dress for her excursion. The first thing she did was to open a large jar of heavy pomade, and slick her chic Italian cut into a good, although obvious imitation of a *pachuco's* ducktail style. With a glance of disdain at the lacy lingerie lining the top drawer of the white and gold dresser, she reached beneath it and pulled out a pair of men's jockey-type shorts. Over these, she donned a pair of clean, tight, fly-front blue jeans. From the same top drawer she located a tight, non-uplift bra, which did its utmost to conceal the curve of her lush breasts. To her continued disgust it failed in the job, but at least it flattened her to some extent. She took a navy blue T-shirt from her closet, pulling it over her head. Standing before the mirror she stretched at the offending garment until it began to hang loosely about her bosom, contributing a bit more to the flat-chested effect she so desired. Marty put on a pair of boy's dark blue socks, over which she added an awesome pair of motorcycle boots. From the dressing table she took a switchblade knife, shoving it into the small front pocket of the jeans, its outline clearly distinguishable.

She walked into her living room and took three ten-dollar bills from her purse, as well as a set of car keys. The keys were for a small car owned by Marty, but registered to another name, at another address. The car registration was the only identification anyone would find on Martha Browning this night.

As she thrust her arms into a black leather jacket it was difficult to recognize the smartly tailored vice president of Amour Cosmetics.

She was no longer Miss Browning. She was Marty, the smartest bull dyke, and the meanest bull dyke, known at

15

"The Song." Dianne Van Lau would have recognized her. It is quite probably that Veronica Ward would not.

For tonight, Marty thought as she walked down the back stairs of the building, I couldn't care less!

She laughed out loud as she thought of the evening ahead.

Chapter III

PROTECTED AND DISGUISED as she was, Marty still looked both ways before she crossed the street to enter the dimly lit "Song." No matter how many times she visited the club, always in search of what one *man* called "quail," she felt this need to check her security first. Sappho's spot—and endless trips to the Board of Supervisors, Courts and other influential tips had failed to allow Sappho to add her own well-given name to "The Song"—still filled Marty with misgivings. It was always after a day such as hers had been, and always when she felt herself falling in love with a new piece of trade, that she was unable to stay away.

As she entered the bar she waved a cheery greeting to the faggot bartender, Bobbie. He was kept on in his job, Marty knew, only as a means of disguising the place to any strange and/or straight person who might visit it mistakenly. The fact that Bobbie hated his customers (the regulars) as much as they hated him failed to hurt business. The dykes and femmes needed a hang-out, and if they had to take a faggot with it—so, they'd take him. At least he didn't despise them as much as a straight cat would.

"Hi, Bobbie. Where's all the usual equipment tonight?" Marty called out as she glanced around the almost empty room.

At the end of the bar, a huge and ugly bull dyke turned to glare at her. At least a portion of her anger could be attributed to the interruption Marty's greeting had been on her big pitch to the drunken stripper she had been so hungrily pawing. "Either stop hollering, baby, or buy the 'equipment' that's here a drink." And, as she slapped the stripper on the behind: "But the drink don't buy no introductions to my new old lady! Got it?"

The bartender tried to look the other way, completely distressed at this opening. He knew Marty as a good spender and one of the few dykes who seemed to be able to avoid trouble. He also knew Gretch, the ugly one at the end of the bar as one of the most officious gals going. He couldn't help hearing the squeal of interest the stripper gave at the sight of Marty, nor the sound of the dyke back-handing her for the insult.

"I can tell you when to squeal, baby. And I can tell you when to look at another dame. You do neither, not until I say so. Until then, you shut up! Got it?"

The stripper, wiping the blood from her cut lip nodded meekly. Marty avoided further discussion by sitting down at the farthest end of the bar and ordering a round for the house. "Tell them it's on the house, Bobbie," she added. "It might keep us both out of trouble."

Bobbie almost said "amen."

Marty nursed her drink, looking around the room as she did so. Dyke though she was, the distinctly sulphuric odor of the place, combined with the inescapable aura of filth, was always distasteful. She watched one of the waitresses serve a couple seated closely in a small booth. The waitress had been with Marty once, and had been a disappointment of the first degree. They didn't speak. Beer, Marty thought to herself. That smell is beer, and stale whiskey, plus disinfectant and a dash of dirty armpits. She suddenly felt depressed beyond reason, and picked up her drink to finish and leave.

Just then the door opened and a strange woman entered—alone.

Marty ordered another round for the house, and watched the "femme" look the place over, then walk to a stool at the bar, not next to Marty. But not too far away.

"Bobbie," Marty spoke softly. "When you have a minute, I'd like to ask you something."

Bobbie nodded, well aware of the forthcoming question. He knew the tip would be a good one if he played his cards right, so he took a little extra time before answering Marty's call. He used it well—and within two minutes of conversation knew exactly for whom the newcomer was whoring, and for what she would settle.

"It's about time, Bobbie," Marty spoke as he finally approached her. "Who's that little pigeon you've got sitting down there? She doesn't look straight, but I've never seen her in here before."

"She's not been around too often," Bobbie replied softly. "I think the first time she came is only a matter of a week or so." He couldn't resist giving a slight dig to Marty —even if she was one of the nicest of them, she was still one of *them*.

"Too bad you weren't around the night she first hit the Song! Honestly, Marty, it was like a bunch of roosters hovering about and fighting over the first little female chicken in the hen yard!"

Marty accepted the dig with a slight smile. It served to anger Bobbie because it reminded him once more of the total failure he'd made in every kind of life he'd attempted. Here he was—one of the most educated and erudite queens in the area. And—*here* he was, tending bar for a bunch of lesbians! Bobbie decided on the spot to mate Marty with the femme. He knew enough about both of them to know in advance they'd have a very ugly ending. That, he thought viciously, will take care of Marty and her superior airs.

None of his thoughts gave visibility to their origin upon his face. But in some strange, almost ESP manner, both Marty and the stranger knew Bobbie had set them up for the scene. They turned their heads away in embarrassment, away from the attraction they'd both felt in the beginning.

Both met emptiness.

Marty ordered another drink.

One, for herself.

The femme ordered one also. For herself.

Bobbie glowed within, and served both. Then he poured one more. For himself.

Gretch, at the other end of the bar, stopped pawing her wife long enough to get a glimpse of the action, which enraged the dyke enough to make her bellow in agony. "Do us no favors, you stupid fag, but when you're pouring drinks, and God knows you don't of'n have time away from your phone calls to your lover to do us the honors—" and she turned for a glance of appreciation from her stripper. The glance she received served to increase her anger. "Goddamnit! We might be 'gay,' but we ain't black! Send us a drink." And in a desperate effort to impress the stripper she'd so recently been pushing around, Gretch ordered a drink, imperiously, "For all the gay gals!"

Marty looked with assumed disgust and expectant empathy toward the new girl. She was met with a pair of deep violet, and very knowing eyes.

Marty decided to move in.

She started by motioning Bobbie to send another drink to the new girl, only this time she gave him a message to deliver with it.

Bobbie almost whistled as he mixed the drink. For a while there he'd thought his plan for a tiny bit of revenge on the world had gone awry. He should have known better than to worry. Marty never came to the Song unless she was hot to trot, and she didn't leave until she'd found a femme to take with her.

"Sorry, honey, but I've forgotten your name," he spoke as he placed the drink carefully before the woman.

"Elizabeth," she answered, almost shyly. "But everyone calls me Betty."

"I won't forget it again, Betty. I've got a friend here, that lady down the bar three stools—this drink is on her. She wants to meet you."

"Is she—is she—you know?"

"What else? Marty's a real butch, but a good one. Never makes trouble, and treats her tricks real good. Okay if I introduce her?"

Betty blushed, but nodded her assent to the liaison. Bobbie grinned, almost triumphantly, and motioned for Marty to move down three stools.

"Betty, this is Marty. Marty, Betty. I think you'll be good for each other. Marty, like I told you, she ain't been around too long, so take it easy on her, huh?"

Marty ignored the remark, turning her full attention to the young woman she'd just met. "Shall we take our drinks over to one of the booths? We might have a little more privacy—" and she stole a sly glance of malice toward Bobbie, "—over there." Betty hesitated a few seconds, then picked up her drink, swung around on the barstool and stood gracefully as she waited for Marty to lead her to a booth. Marty took the drink from her hand and grabbing her own drink from the bar, walked in proud cavalier fashion to one of the dim booths in the back of the room. She felt quite superior as she passed the other occupants of the room. Betty was obviously the catch of the evening, and Marty had caught her.

"Finish your drink, honey," she ordered Betty with quiet confidence. "We'll have one more before we go."

"Go?"

"Go," Marty said with a flat tone of emphasis. "Now

21

that I've met you, I want to know you *better*. You do understand?"

Betty blushed again, but wasn't so confused that she forgot her reason for agreeing to the introduction. She might have been new to the Song, but she had an old lady with a huge appetite for money. Betty hadn't joined forces with her more than three days before she'd been sent out on the streets to get some for her. "I think I do, Marty. But I don't know. You see, I'm almost broke, and—"

"And I'm old enough to know you never get something for nothing! Okay? You just name the price, there'll be no arguments. But right now, let's forget it. For just a little while let's pretend it's a matter of love instead of money. Agreed?"

Betty was still new enough at the game to go along with Marty's temporizing of the issue. She gulped down her drink as instructed and, when the lesbian waitress answered Marty's call, gave her order for another one.

"My, my," the les said facetiously, "you two seem to be hitting it off nobly. You both want a drink, or is it just the one?"

"The one." Marty's voice was sullen.

"Yes, *sir*." The waitress had gotten her message.

As she left the table to fill the order, Marty reached beneath it and patted Betty's soft thigh. "Tell me, little Betty," she added, as her fingers trailed slightly higher, insinuating, exploring, demanding, "just how long have you been 'one of us'?"

The caressing hand was disturbingly exciting to the young girl, and she was slightly breathless as she replied, "Not quite a month. And I love it. Do you think—well, does my enjoyment seem awful to you? I mean, I thought I was straight for so long, and maybe you think it isn't right for me to change so suddenly—and so completely?"

"Look, baby Betty. Why should I think you're awful? The only awful thing is that you didn't join us long ago. After all, what you do is your own business, isn't it? That's your body you're playing around with. And incidentally," the exploring hand was removed gently as the waitress approached their booth with the lone drink on her tray, "you—and your body—bother me tremendously."

Betty started to gasp her answer, but held the words back as the waitress reached the booth and put the drink on the table in front of her. Marty didn't take her eyes from the young girl as she reached into a pocket of her jeans and threw a bill on the tray, muttering to the waitress to "keep the change but get lost in a hurry." The les threw a "thanks" over her shoulder as she scurried back to her station at the bar, hurrying to get away before Marty realized the bill had been a five. She wasn't three feet way before Marty's hand was once more under the table, taking up her caressing where she'd left off before.

"Please, Marty—" If Betty was simulating her passion she was doing a damned good job of it, Marty thought to herself—"I'm getting awfully excited. Please wait until we leave— Oh, no," she continued breathlessly, "no, that's so beautiful . . ."

Marty was beginning to join Betty in her quick emotions, and was glad she'd stopped by and rented that little motel room before she'd arrived at the Song. The quicker they got there, the quicker Marty could give vent to the passions which had been building within her throughout the day. She'd left two bottles in the room; one Scotch and one gin. "Come on, baby-girl. Finish your drink and let's get out of here. I want you so much it's pathetic. And I'm getting tired of waiting."

"Let's forget the drink," gasped Betty. "I want you just as much as you want me. I hope your pad isn't too far. I mean—can we get where we're going in a hurry?"

"Really got you on fire, huh?"

"Oh, sweet daddy, yes! Yes! Yes! Take me out of here, now!"

Marty stood up, and helped Betty out of the booth. Her eyes were heavy-lidded with passion. As the girl crossed in front of her, Marty's hands moved with evil insinuation across Betty's breasts, feeling the sweet erectness of her young nipples. The violence of Betty's response was a delight and a shock to Marty. She removed her hands hastily, fearful that a novice like this might truly be unable to wait.

The two women looked neither to left nor right as they hurried across the barroom and out the front door. And neither of them heard the raucous laughter of Gretch and her stripper as it sailed insultingly across the room behind them.

The Song was packed by the time Betty got back. Gretch and the stripper were completely swacked, and paying little or no attention to the other customers as they fondled and pinched one another. The faggot bartender was in a sweat, more because of their actions than the exercise he was getting from the heavy business of the evening. Man, he thought to himself, if the fuzz ever walks in here now, Sappho will get busted for sure. But he wasn't about to try to break the two apart. He'd seen Gretch in a drunken fury, and knew beyond doubt that she could flatten him in five seconds, and probably would if he said anything to her.

Betty sat alone at the other end of the bar, trying to contain the tears which kept fighting their way to her eyes. When Bobbie finally spotted her, he knew without being told what had happened. But he walked down to Betty anyhow.

"How'd it go, Betts? She's a great butch, didn't I tell you?"

"Bobbie," Betty leaned over the bar, whispering in a choked voice, "I don't know what to do. She was a great lover, you were right about that. And honestly, Bobbie, I did everything she wanted me to do, and let her do everything to me that she wanted to do. But when we were finished, and I asked her for my money, she—" and fright-

24

ened tears began to pour down Betty's face, as Bobbie supplied the end of her sentence for her.

"—she wouldn't pay off?"

Betty nodded, still unable to control her tears.

"Kee-rist, chickie, do you mean to tell me you didn't learn the first night that in your racket you either get the money first, or you don't get it at all?"

Betty finally regained control of herself enough to go on with her story. "I didn't think *she* would be like that."

"They're all like that, and you should know it by now!"

"But what'll I tell my old lady? She'll beat the devil out of me if I come home without any loot—particularly when she finds out I went off with a trick. And she'll find that out. You know how the gossip goes around in this place. Bobbie, could you—would you lend me ten bucks? I promise I'll pay it back out of my next few tricks."

"No chance, Betty. If I lent you anything I'd have every femme in the place crying on my shoulder for loot." The fag looked around the room thoughtfully, and as his eyes hit upon Gretch and her stripper, he said a silent prayer of thanks to Marty for sending Betty back without any money. "Look, baby. Gretch and that new broad of hers have been playing around with each other so long they're bound to be getting bored. Why don't you go over to them and offer to run interference?"

Betty looked at him, puzzled. "Interference? I don't understand."

"Your old lady didn't train you very well, did she? You go over to those two and tell them they've gotten you all riled up, watching their action. Offer to let them take turns with you, if they'll take you to their pad *right now*. Gretch is an ugly bull-dyke, but she's loaded with loot. So, incidentally, is her stripper—at least, she is tonight."

"Do you think they'll—?"

"I know damned good and well they will. They might have laughed you and Marty out of the bar, but you could

25

hear the jealousy in both of them. They hate Marty. Don't tell them she stiffed you, and they'll think they're getting back at her."

Betty nodded her understanding, and stood up to head for the two at the other end of the bar. As she walked toward them she heard Bobbie's voice calling behind her; "This time, Betts, get the loot *first*."

She did.

Chapter IV

THE WAR that burst into being when Veronica broke the news of her new job to Kirk was a ring-a-ding. The first battle was rowdy and vituperative, ending only when the two protagonists were so exhausted that they were unable to continue. By that time, the vituperation was at least five lengths ahead of everything else.

Veronica had expected some form of antagonism from Kirk but had been amazed at the strength of his feelings against her proposal. He, in turn, had been amazed at her stubborn insistence on continuing with her project.

By the next morning the hot war had dissolved itself into a cold war of curt statements and little communication.

By Monday, both sides had maintained an "Okay, we'll wait and see what happens" attitude, and Veronica arrived at the swank Sunset Strip office, excited but wearied from a weekend of marital combat.

Marty Browning was there to greet her.

Following Martha's venture into the murky depths of The Song that Thursday night, she had spent a day repenting the quirk in her nature that made such excursions necessary from time to time. The balance of her weekend had been devoted to working over some feasible plan of making her pet project, the Movie Starlet line of cheap cosmetics more palatable to the New York office. Veronica Wade, she had decided, was going to become part of that project. Her social prestige would be used as a selling point. For the time being, Martha had also decided to adopt a strictly hands-off attitude toward her new employee. In keeping with her decisions, she had called the secretarial pool for a girl to occupy the receptionist job originally set aside for Veronica. The girl, a rather plain and mousy person was tremendously impressed with this chance to work with the vice-president, and was at the desk when Veronica came in.

"Conference," Martha said curtly. "Let's go into my office." She turned to address the plain girl, "Please call the art department and tell Lisa I want to see her and her three top people; to report here within the next half hour. With," she added grimly, "the new layouts for Movie Starlet." She walked into her office without waiting for the girl to place the call. Veronica followed, firmly repressing a girlish giggle of self-impressed importance.

Veronica was told to sit down and listen. As Martha began to explain the change in plans, she paced up and down, speaking at times curtly, then rapidly, but constantly selling Veronica on the importance of her role in the new campaign.

"New York," explained Martha, "is as blind and stubborn at this point as the blindest and most stubborn of all jackasses! They can't get it through their heads that my idea for a line of cheaper cosmetics won't in any way affect their pet 'Amour' goodies. They seem to think we'll lose our expensive customers because we'll be underselling ourselves. They also seem to think the campaign we've set up is without 'taste and integrity.' Oh," she whirled to face Veronica, who sat listening in fascinated silence, "they want the money we can make with Movie Starlet. But they want to have their gin and drink it too! Will you help me with this, Mrs. Wade? Will you go along with my new ideas? Will—" and Martha was really anxious about this point, "—will your husband have any objections to your taking part in it? The use of your picture, name, and so on?"

Veronica shook her head by way of negative reply, thinking to herself that Kirk would blow his stack. He'd been angry enough when her plan had consisted of merely an office job to remove some of the boredom from her life. When he found out that it had changed to being model, television sales-woman, and endorser of a thing to be known as "Movie Starlet Cosmetics"—wow! However, Veronica wasn't about to have her certain knowledge of his reactions endanger her chances of having the fun this campaign promised. She already fancied herself signing autographs.

Martha, relieved at her assenting to the complete revision of last Thursday's meeting, walked over to her desk and pushed down the button on the intercom. "Have you reached the art department?"

"I was just about to announce them, Miss Browning," came back the reply, in a plain voice that matched the face of its speaker.

"Send them in." Martha smiled as she spoke, flipping the button on the ugly little machine. When the four women entered, each carrying a new set of layouts, each nervous in her own particular way, Martha was still smiling. It was, thought Veronica to herself, an almost sadistic smile.

She soon found out she was right.

Marty might be having her problems with the head office at this point, but in spite of them she remained the fair-haired girl of the West Coast operation. Marty intended to keep that status. Her own personal problems gave her an insight into the man-woman relationship that the rather more "normal" idea people back east couldn't possibly match. She knew her advantage and she made damned good use of it.

"Now, Lisa," she attacked the art director frontally,

29

"have you found out what *you* did—you, and your assistants—to dissuade New York against the Movie Starlet line? I sold them on the idea, you know." Marty began to pace again, long slim legs decisively placed as she took each new stride. "And I don't like the idea of the weak campaign you worked out ruining the entire deal. Are *you*—" she swung to face the defenseless art director, "perhaps as lazy, or prejudiced against the entire idea as *they* were in the beginning? Too much trouble—maybe even a bit of snobbishness rearing its ugly head?"

Lisa bit her lips in an attempt to hold back the retort she felt was fairly deserved by the other woman. She softened it somewhat, but not entirely. "It wasn't my campaign—nor my *fault*—and you know it. I've never shirked my work, Miss Browning, and I've never failed to satisfy New York when you let *me* do it!"

Marty's eyes were flashing warning signals for her art director to shut up, but a weekend of worrying about the injustice of her situation had made Lisa blind to everything but just that.

"I didn't like the idea in the beginning, true. But I told you exactly how I felt—I told you in private—not," she glanced pointedly at Veronica, then toward her assistants, "I repeat—*not* in front of a group of other Amour employees!"

"I think," there was no doubting the authority in Marty's voice, "we should leave that discussion until later. For now, let me see what you've come up with this time. If you don't mind showing me in front of 'other Amour employees.' "

Veronica didn't know where to look, so played it safe and looked at the floor. For a fleeting second she wished she'd paid more attention to Kirk and turned down this job. During that second though, she also remembered the restless nights, the unhappy days, the fact that this morning—in fact all of the time since her first meeting with Marty—the boredom had been dissipated. She

30

watched cautiously as Marty (Miss Browning, she reminded herself) glanced contemptuously at each layout handed her by the now sweating Lisa. She tossed them each with equal contempt in the general direction of the wastebasket.

Marty threw the last layout toward its grave beside the others then turned back to Lisa, speaking softly. "You've missed the point entirely. Perhaps it will change your entire concept of my new line if you learn that Mrs. Veronica Ward," she pointed in dramatic style toward the mesmerized witness to this first insight into 'big-business-operations,' "is not only going to endorse 'Movie Starlet,' but is also going to make television commercials, as well as posing for magazine and newspaper advertisements. You think, or have thought that just because these are cheaper cosmetics, they deserve only the cheapest of selling campaigns. That's not the way to look at it." Now Marty was selling Lisa and her assistants, as hard as she had earlier sold Veronica, on her new idea. "You have to look at it as though it's an entirely new business. Forget Amour. Forget lipsticks and face creams that cost as much as a bottle of champagne or a gigolo for the night! You have to remember the millions of lower-income women who might not be able to afford a bottle of 'New Affair' perfume, but damned good and well want to buy anything they can to bring some truck driver around to the point of supporting them! And you have to remember that Veronica Ward is—to those women— the *elite* of the elite! With her saying Movie Starlet will bring the men around, those millions of women aren't going to doubt it. Not only is Ronnie—as they call it— 'high-society' she's also one of the few women in this country who divorced a millionaire and married a billionaire! All without scandal!"

Lisa and her assistants were listening to Marty with an almost worshipping attitude. Their scruples had raised their ugly heads, but once again Marty Browning had spotted the fault, and found the only possible answer. She had out-thought them. She had sold them on a line in which they had never had the slightest bit of faith. Her line, but of this they hadn't the slightest bit of knowledge —Movie Starlet.

Lisa voiced their unspoken thoughts. "I have to apologize for all of us, Miss Browning. We realize—" She didn't glance toward Veronica, but did indicate her knowledge of her presence (and her importance) by a hand flung quickly in her general direction, "—with someone such as Mrs. Ward behind us, naturally any question as to the lack of quality, or of ethics or of good taste—well, to put it briefly, a question would be out of the question, no?"

"Start with that as a premise." Marty jumped on the phrase. "Something along the line of 'to question the appeal and the beauty of Mrs. Veronica Ward would be out of the question.' Then move on to her own pitch— which we'll write for you—she'll recommend our Movie Starlet. And she'll convince every woman that listens or watches her that she enjoys it, and isn't *above* saving her money by purchasing such good, but inexpensive beauty products!"

Marty had become so excited by the reaction of the art director to her idea of using Ronnie in the campaign that she was almost scrambling for her words. She still had a mudpack to throw at Lisa and her assistants. It was going to take a long time for the sting of that New York call to leave her; the knowledge that Lisa and her assistants were the only people in the organization who knew that Marty was solely responsible for the debacle of the original campaign was the only reason she hadn't already flung it. However, not only are love and hate akin. A few other emotions go into that same category. Dislike, distrust, and expediency should never be confused. Marty might be annoyed with them, but Lisa and her women were going to end up as some of her strongest allies in her fight to see New York bow down to the wishes of Martha Browning, V.P. She had no sexual designs on any of the women. Physically not one of them was attractive to her. But she knew how she could use them, and now that she'd enlisted Veronica, she intended to use them frequently.

Marty had worked long and hard for her money. She had hopes of becoming independently wealthy so that she could live a life without fear—a life wherein her strange desires and stranger methods of practicing her wants could never jeopardize her bank account. The Movie Starlet idea was a giant step toward her goal—so important that Marty had brought herself to part with a goodly chunk of dough, investing it all in Amour Cosmetics. For it, she hoped to receive a high percentage of profits. She glanced at Ronnie Ward who sat watching the scene in delighted amazement. To herself, Marty thought, she's not only good for my ego, she's going to be a helluva help to my economic status. She put the thought out of her mind and returned to the point at hand.

"Okay, go back to your art department, Lisa, and let's see you lay out some really hard-hitting stuff for me. Don't make any detailed layouts though. Just give me a bunch of suggestions with some rough sketches, and we'll play it by ear from there. I want you to come up with something intriguing, forceful. And, ladies,"—Marty couldn't resist one little dig on the vengeful side—"I want them in good taste. Shall we say, 'almost aristocratic'?"

Her arrow missed the target. Lisa and her ladies were already hard at work, so they took the remark with good grace. They swept out of her office smiling, all of them filled with a new sense of excitement and enthusiasm.

Marty ran a well manicured hand through her smoothly coiffed hair then flopped down on the long, dark green leather couch directly across the room from Veronica. For at least five minutes, although it did seem much longer to Ronnie, Marty lay there, staring up at the ceiling, deep in thought.

She finally turned to stare at Veronica.

"Do you prefer to use your own wardrobe?"

The question caught Ronnie by surprise. For a moment she failed to understand Marty.

"In the TV commercials," Marty added. "Do you want to use your own clothes or shall we go out and buy you a new television wardrobe? We'd want to keep it simple, yet elegant, a modified version of Loretta Young. You see, Ronnie, these women are going to have to 'identify' with you. They'll envy and want to emulate you. That's quite understandable, don't you think?"

Ronnie nodded silently, her mind racing through her many, mirrored closets, accepting this gown as perfect for her new role, rejecting another as perhaps a bit too chi-chi.

"Of course," Marty continued, "if you do decide to wear your own gowns—and I think, at this point, it might be best if you'll do so—we'll replace them later. You would continue to work with your own dressmaker, no?"

"Yes," Ronnie mused, "yes, I think you're right. I've already decided on four outfits I think meet your description almost perfectly—what was it? Simple, yet elegant?"

Marty sat up on the couch, reaching for a cigarette as she did so. She caressed the jade lighter as she picked it up from the coffee table in front of her and flicked the wheel.

"We'll have to give you one of your own makeup men. A specialist in the field. You wear very little makeup, I've noticed, and you look just about perfect for street, restaurant and office. But it's different under the lights, you know. We'll have to cover that lovely complexion with all kinds of things. I think I'll use Eric for the job. He's just about tops, and he'll fall absolutely in love with your facial angles. He's gay, but a great man at his work. You don't mind, do you?"

"Mind?" Ronnie caught the last few words, but had been concentrating upon her selection of wardrobe, and actually not paying close attention to Marty's quick-spoken words.

"The gay bit."

My God, Ronnie thought to herself. Has she been sitting there making a verbal pass at me while I've been sitting over here thinking about something else entirely?

"I don't," she spoke hesitantly, "I don't quite understand."

"Oh, come off it, Ronnie," Marty laughed, taking a deep drag of her cigarette as she finished. "You certainly know what a 'gay' man is. I merely want to know if you'll mind having one of them work on your face."

"Oh, of course not, Miss Browning," Ronnie answered in quick relief.

"Make it 'Marty,'" her employer added. "The 'Miss Browning' bit was all right when you were going to be nothing but a receptionist around the place. But as the star member of the Movie Starlet advertising campaign, you're one of us. That makes it strictly a first-name relationship. Right?"

"If you say so—Marty."

"I've just said so. Now, you take the rest of the day off. Go home, go through your clothes and pick out everything you think might be right for the TV spots. We won't use them all, but give us a choice. I'll have one of our drivers at your place in the morning to pick them up."

Ronnie stood hesitantly. Somehow it didn't seem the right thing to do—to leave the office so early on her very first day of work.

Marty read her mind, and laughed once again.

"Don't worry, Ronnie. Think of all the time you're

really saving us. If we had to have a new wardrobe designed and made up for you, hell, it would be weeks before we could get started."

Rising, she walked over to her desk and jabbed the cigarette out in a large ashtray. Then she walked across the room and put an arm fondly around Ronnie's shoulder. "There'll be some nights, baby, that I'll keep you working so long you'll be ready to fall on your face. Some nights when you won't even have the energy to go home! When those times come, remember this first and very short day. It might make it easier for you.

"Now, I've got a few more than a million and one things to do, so take off. Quick, Ronnie, before I have you thrown out!"

Ronnie was startled by the gruff-sounding words, but then noticed the laughter lurking in Marty's eyes. She gave her new boss a cheerful salute, and walked out of the office.

It was to be the last time in a long time that Ronnie left Marty so early.

Chapter V

MISS BRADLEY WAS FORTY-ISH, unattractive and efficient. She loved God, the United States, the Methodist church, the Republican party, and her boss, Kirk Ward.

But only Mr. Ward could do no wrong. This was an honest opinion and one which she'd formed with much soul-searching. She was Mr. Ward's secretary, sent to him from the agency pool. From the first, he'd trusted her implicitly, confided in her. No one in the world (she thought, wrongly) knew his innermost thoughts as well as she.

Today, she knew that Mr. Ward was preoccupied, almost distressed. Although Miss Bradley was currently the victim of the flu bug, and had gone through half a box of tissues by nine-thirty, and had almost requested the day off, one look at Mr. Ward had changed her mind. Her complaint, after all, was only some virus that was making the rounds at the television studios. Kirk (she called him that privately, never to his face) on the other hand, had some real trouble. This gave her a certain amount of satisfaction. Not that she wanted him to ever have any trouble, but she was more than ready to help however she might. God knows the television wolves were never very far from the doorstep. Well, here was *one* office they weren't getting past today!

Primly, she patted her nose with a fresh tissue, wincing at the tenderness of her nostrils.

She rearranged some papers on her desk, then got the mail ready to take in to Mr. Ward's office. Her buzzer sounded. She picked up the telephone, and pressed the "intercom" button.

"Yes, Mr. Ward?"

"Come in, please, Miss Bradley." She thought he sounded as if the weight of the world was upon his shoulders, as indeed it often was. The poor, dear man. Who'd dare put him in such a mood? Indignantly, Miss Bradley gathered up the mail and a sheaf of notes and went, radiantly, albeit sniffingly, into Kirk's office. This was always the brightest spot of her day. Everything after this was downhill. In a way, it was Miss Bradley's morning ritual rather than morning routine. She woke to it, looking forward to it with a sort of maidenly expectancy.

Kirk looked up scowling as Miss Bradley swept into the room. He said nothing as she picked up some "out" papers, deposited some "in" papers, carefully placed the day's mail on his desk, then opened her new steno pad (Ward insisted on a fresh one every day, and she took the old one home and burned it at night, because he disliked having notes tossed into the wastebasket) and sat down in her chair, smiling helpfully.

Kirk opened the first letter, scanned it and began dictating. He'd first been dismayed then overjoyed at the fates that had sent Miss Bradley to his office. Unlike many of the beautiful young things that his colleagues gladly accepted, Miss Bradley was the perpetual bodyguard. She fended off unwelcome visitors, was impervious to gifts, flattery or threats. She protected Kirk and she was confident that he'd protect her, as indeed he had. She was loyal to a fault, and if she had a weakness, it was in her admiration for him. Of these things, although he'd never voiced them, he was still aware. He had no pet name for her, calling her only Miss Bradley. But she always received a handsome check and a gift on her birthday, and at Christmas he doubled the network bonus and included another gift for her. At a financial cost of perhaps five hundred dollars a year, then, he had the gem of the stenographer's pool. He'd also pushed through a few raises for her. She would have given her life for him, and he was somewhat amusedly aware of it. Ordinarily, he would "rib" her at this morning session, laughing inwardly at her pink cheeks. This morning was an exception. He didn't feel happy. He was, he told himself, not unhappy without reason. Sensitive to his attitudes, Miss Bradley sat quietly, only an occasional sniffle betraying her presence.

Looking at Ward as he sat there, glumly going through his mail, one would have been hard put to it to figure why he was unhappy. He was reasonably young, worked at a job he enjoyed, had a beautiful wife. By astute management, wise investment and a few breaks, he was several times over a millionaire. Handsome, popular, a man's man and a woman's dream.

He commended loyalty from his subordinates, admiration from his rivals, respect from his few enemies. His word was as good as a contract, chiefly because he never gave his word unless a contract was in process of being signed. He showered daily, wore good clothing well, if a bit carelessly. He belonged to the right clubs, played a good hand of bridge and a dangerous if somewhat reckless game of gin. He drank his bourbon neat or on the rocks. He had a normal amount of vanity about his success, but had been a crashing failure once, so that he knew he was always walking a tightrope. If he had a fault, it was his generosity, but he didn't often allow it to run away with him. He was witty, well-read, and turned down more party invitations than he accepted.

He was the perfect, well-rounded male.

He was also, he realized, a crashing bore to his wife.

He handed the sheaf of mail to Miss Bradley. "Routine. Answer 'em, and I'll sign later." She nodded. "I'm going out for a few hours. I'll call to see if there's anything extra urgent. By 'urgent' today, I mean if the FCC should knock the network off the air. Handle things for me."

She got to her feet. "Yes, sir." She was pleased at this trust.

Ward waited until she'd left the room, then went to the little bar in one corner of his plush office, took out an Old-Fashioned glass and a bottle of bonded bourbon. He started to pour a stiff one, then reconsidered and put back the bottle and glass.

Whatever his problems, liquor wouldn't solve them. Indeed, the way he felt today, liquor would undoubtedly enlarge them. Also, on work days, at least—and lately that had been six and often seven days a week—he disliked drinking in the morning. Bad habit.

He locked his desk, went out through a private door and down to the parking lot, still pondering what course of action to take. While he waited for the attendant to bring his car, Kirk decided to run out to Malibu and take a look at his summer home. The sea air would do him good. He knew when he and Ronnie spent much of their time at the ocean—without even the company of servants—he relaxed, almost completely.

He got into his car, and drove west on Sunset Boulevard. He scowled as he endured the stop-and-go traffic along the Strip, then relaxed a bit as he entered Beverly Hills, holding his speed to forty miles an hour. Now he could think again.

Why? His mind kept repeating the question, just as he'd repeated it to Veronica throughout the long, miserable weekend. Why? Why did she want to take a flunkie job with a miserable cosmetics firm? It wasn't for the money involved, obviously. Forgetting the enormous settlement she'd received from her first husband—forgetting all the blue-chip stocks and coupon clipping which

40

added to her personal account, Kirk gave her a monthly salary that approached extravagance—far more, he was certain than the salary she'd mentioned. Also, he suspected, she'd blown up the size of her salary. He knew Amour Cosmetics. The net had carried some of their commercials, which weren't particularly good, to Kirk. There'd also been rumors from some of the agency boys that the firm was in financial trouble. The fact that Ronnie had told him they were going to enter the field of cheaper cosmetics would seem to indicate the truth of the rumors. What was that awful name they'd come up with? Kirk couldn't remember, but it had left a bad taste in his mouth.

Was it possible that Ronnie was doing this because of sheer boredom? He shook his head impatiently as he entered the Palisades. How could that be? She had more than enough to keep her occupied. Junior League, several charities, a popular and very-much-in-demand chairlady for several philanthropic organizations. Then there was her Girls' Club thing and her hospital committee. That, plus managing their large home—two homes, really— her appointments at the beauty salon, her twice-weekly schedule at the gymnasium to keep her fine figure in trim and trips to her dressmaker. Hell, Kirk thought, she maintains a schedule that would kill a horse! It simply couldn't be boredom.

He turned right where Sunset Boulevard joined the Pacific Coast Highway, drove steadily for some twenty minutes, enjoying the speed of the car now that he was able to open it up a little, and sniffing appreciatively of the salt air. He turned into the drive of his beach house, parked and got out, stretching.

Suddenly the morning looked beautiful to him. He took off his jacket, tossed it into the back seat, unloosened his tie, turned up his shirt sleeves, unlocked the door and walked through the house to the back. He decided that he'd have a drink after all. With difficulty he managed to get a tray of ice cubes from the refrigerator, remembering as he did so that he'd neglected to turn the thing to "defrost" the last time they'd been out. He didn't turn it to "defrost" this time, either.

Kirk poured himself a stiff drink, dropped one ice cube into it, then slid open the glass wall of the living room and went out to the patio, stretching out in a comfortable deck chair.

He took a sip from his drink, then another. Closing his eyes he lay back and tried to remember the details of the ugly quarrel that had extended from Thursday night through Saturday, then Sunday and even up until this morning at breakfast. By then the original fireworks had fizzled down to an unspectacular but very cold war. What had started it?

That was easy enough to answer. When she'd announced brightly, and Kirk had realized immediately with the false gaiety of an afternoon gin-drinker, that she was accepting a "position" with the Amour Cosmetics firm, he'd glanced at her to see if she was kidding. It was obvious that she was not.

"You're *what?*"

She'd gone on to explain. She was to act as recep— well, she'd hedged, "consultant" to the vice president, and she'd continued describing the opportunity in glowing terms, ignoring his "What the hell do *you* know about cosmetics? You don't even wear them! A consultant has to know everything about manufacturing, marketing, the works." Ronnie continued blithely. Her duties, she reiterated, would entail working directly beneath a Martha Browning, their vice president in charge of West Coast operations. Kirk had no definite knowledge that Ronnie was exaggerating, but his educated guess to that effect was a good one.

And having reached that conclusion, Kirk proceeded to blow his top.

"Do you," he'd asked coldly, "have the slightest idea

what you're saying? Even a vague idea of what you're planning to do to that poor cosmetic company? Or, do I have to spell it out for you? Forget it, Ronnie. Forget the whole thing. Stick to your varied charities—keep on doing good deeds for the natives. *But stay the hell away from that cosmetics factory.* Leave the business world to that ugliest of your species—the business women. And that, my darling wife, is an order!"

Ronnie hadn't answered him, but had run crying from the room. He'd gone to the bar and poured himself another drink.

Kirk opened his eyes, watched the sandpipers running in and out before the surf as if they were on tracks. He decided to have another drink now, too. Several drinks later he changed into a pair of slacks and a comfortable beach shirt. His polished shoes had been removed in favor of a pair of canvas sneakers. He felt relaxed, fairly drunk and extremely unhappy. Also, he felt the need for some companionship.

He got in the car, backed out and drove down the highway to his favorite beach bar, The Key.

"Hey, look who just came in," he was greeted by Johnny O'Shea, the bartender, with the familiarity of long acquaintanceship. "And on Monday, too! Playin' hookey from the network, hey?"

"In a way. And I think I'll start off the festivities with a bottle of beer. Okay, Irishman? And, John, here—take my car keys. I may get very, very drunk. If I do, I don't want to be driving."

"Sure." O'Shea put the keys in his pocket and brought Kirk's beer. He looked at the network official with anxiety written on his honest face. "None of my business, Kirk, but what is it? Family trouble?"

Kirk sipped at his beer, gratefully tasting its coolness. "You could say that. At least I'm afraid there's going to be." He tossed a bill on the bar. "Get me some telephone change, will you? I'd better call my office."

He had to go through the operator, and finally deposited thirty-five cents before he heard Miss Bradley's voice. No, nothing vital had come up. Nothing that couldn't wait until morning. Yes, Mrs. Ward had called an hour ago, left the message that she was leaving her office on some outside business. Miss Bradley read the line perfectly, with just a slight overtone of question in her voice. He glanced at the dial, gave the number of The Key and said he'd be there during the work day in case some real emergency came up. He hung up, went back to the bar, shoved the beer back and called for a double bourbon on the rocks.

The other customer in the bar had gone.

O'Shea brought Kirk's drink, setting it before him silently.

"No change," Kirk told him. "It's still a lousy situation."

"Help to talk about it, Kirk? It won't go any further, you know that."

"I don't know. Have a drink yourself."

"Why not?" Johnny grinned. "Do me a world of good."

Kirk told the story, in detail, downing another double as he did so. The bartender listened and made sympathetic noises throughout the narration.

"So," Kirk concluded, "I'm at a dead end."

Johnny nodded. "Women! Who can understand 'em? I tell you what, though—it's none of my business, but I don't see so much harm in it. It's probably just a phase she's going through. And then you working such long hours and being out of town a lot and all that. You can get lonesome in a crowd, you know."

Lonesome in a crowd!

Was that it? That had to be it. Sure. Same old faces, same old benefits and bazaars, same cocktail parties, same round of social events.

"John, my good buddy, you might have something there."

O'Shea beamed. "Damned right. Listen, I *know* Ronnie, remember. She's a wonderful girl, and she loves you. I can tell. A bartender learns to spot the phonies from a hundred yards. That girl's got class. No, sir, she just wants to kick up her heels a little bit and do something interesting, something challenging."

Kirk suddenly felt better. He grinned. "Let's have another drink, John. This one's for a more cheerful outlook. Okay. I don't like what she's doing, but I agree; it'll wear off after the novelty wears off."

That drink led to another and yet another. And another. O'Shea's night relief man came on duty. Johnny, feeling no pain himself by now, joined Kirk at the bar "for just one more," then slipped to the telephone.

"He's all right, Ronnie. This is Johnny O'Shea at The Key. He's a little under the weather, but he's finally decided to live with the idea of your working. Trouble is, we're both too drunk to drive. What I'll do, I'll take him up to your beach house by cab. I'll put the car keys in the medicine cabinet. He'll be asleep before you can get out here, so take your time. What? Forget it, honey. Any time."

He hung up, called a Malibu cab, went back into the bar and had yet another "roader" with Kirk. The cab came, Johnny said, "Well, let's up and at 'em, kid," and Kirk obediently followed him out.

They arrived at the beach house at about seven-thirty. O'Shea told the driver he'd be right back, to wait. He helped a stumbling Kirk into the house and out of his clothing and onto the king-sized bed. Kirk promptly started snoring. Johnny shook his head, admiringly. God! he thought, what a pad!

He went to the bar and poured himself a drink. On second thought, he picked up an unopened bottle, stuffed it into his waistband, under his coat. He started to leave, turned back and, going into the bath, dropped Kirk's keys into the medicine cabinet. With owlish gravity he

45

made sure the spring lock was working on the front door as he pulled it to after him.

"You know him, huh?" the cab driver asked as they swung onto the highway. "A real big shot."

Johnny patted the bottle under his jacket. "Know him? Hell, he's a drinking buddy of mine. One of the best guys ever walking. We're just like—*that*." He attempted to indicate with his fingers just how they were, but the fingers weren't coordinating so well.

Later, perhaps two or three hours later, the front door of the Wards' Malibu home opened, and Ronnie slipped in, quietly. She slipped off her clothing, tossed an overnight bag onto a chair, and climbed in quietly beside her husband, this man she loved so dearly and yet from whom she obtained so little satisfaction. He wakened gradually, puzzled at first, not knowing where he was and wondering what Ronnie was doing with him.

He lay quietly, considering. He remembered O'Shea's advice, and quite suddenly a warm wave of tenderness toward this woman swept over him.

He murmured her name. "Ronnie, darling. I'm sorry."

She'd been dozing off, exhausted by her day, but she was instantly awake, knowing he loved her, knowing he was apologizing like a little boy for his actions over the weekend and his solitary drunk of today. Tears came to her eyes and she moved close to him.

No other words were spoken as he caressed her lovely body, showing her his need for her. She opened herself to receive him, to accept his love. Only once did she make a noise, and that was a small climactic cry that was immediately echoed by some night-flying bird just outside the open glass doors. It was one of their better love-making experiences.

Afterwards, they lit cigarettes and, by mutual consent, didn't speak. Things were fine.

Finally Kirk spoke. "I'm going to have one more drink. To sort of welcome myself back to the fold."

46

He switched on the bedside lamp and climbed out of bed. Ronnie found herself admiring his body. He was still a fine-looking man. In fact, she thought, we're a fine-looking couple. She didn't particularly approve of the drink, but decided to be a sport about it.

"Me, too," she said, pushing back the covers and making a rush for the bathroom.

He chuckled warmly, fixing their drinks. As a "consultant," he thought, she'd be invaluable to her firm. Privately, he gave her a month, at the outside, to disentangle her dainty person from the web of commerce.

She returned from the bathroom, clad in a pair of towels. "I thought I had a robe in there," she complained. "I wonder whatever happened to it?"

"I think that outfit is very becoming. Let's take our drinks out on the deck, darling." He grabbed a pack of cigarettes up from the little night table beside the bed, and taking the drinks in one hand led the way through the French window onto the deck. The air was cool, but not yet cold, and the sound and smell of the ocean complimented their mood. They sat side by side, companionably.

Kirk lit a cigarette for Ronnie, then one for himself. They took long drags from their smokes, and sipped their drinks in silence. Kirk looked at the stars in the clear, smog-free sky. A meteorite flashed briefly across the dimly-visible horizon.

Star light, star bright, Kirk intoned mentally. "Well, darling, how was your first day in the outside world?"

"Better than I expected, to tell you the truth, Kirk. But, darling, are you sure you want to talk about it—now? I mean, you've been so upset the past few days . . ."

"The *past* few days, Ronnie. And you're right, I was very upset." He made a wry face in the dark. "It took—it's still taking, a little getting used to—the idea of having a wife who's working as a 'consultant' for a cosmetics

47

firm. Still, I'm learning to live with it. If it's what you want to do, you're certainly entitled to do it. After all, you've never tried to tell me—"

"Oh," Ronnie interrupted, knowing that Kirk would be proud of her, "it's developing into something much more important than just a consultant's job. A real, fun kind of thing.

"Marty Browning, you know—the vice-president—explained her new plans to me this morning. I tried to reach you at the office to tell you about it, but you'd gone out. You see, they're about to break into the market with this new line, the Movie Starlet thing, and—"

"Get to the point, Ronnie," Kirk said uneasily, "what's this 'much more important' job?"

"I've been selected by Marty to be the model for the campaign. And more than that, I'm also going to do their commercials. Can't you see me walking into the living rooms of the world!"

Kirk sat upright in the deck chair. "You *what?*" he exploded. "I hope to God you had sense enough to say no to a stupid idea like that! Did it ever occur to you that this 'important job' of yours could put my neck on the chopping block? It isn't bad enough that you have to hire yourself out to work for a third-rate cosmetics manufacturer who, if the Madison Avenue rumors are correct, is on the verge of bankruptcy. But now you have to accept a silly role as television 'hostess' for a company that just happens to buy time *on a rival network!* Isn't there a brain left in that lovely little head of yours?"

Kirk reached over and grasped Ronnie's hand. "Don't you see that what you're suggesting verges on lunacy? You can imagine what the network brass will have to say to me about *this!*"

"They'd be pretty narrow-minded if they said anything about it!" Ronnie retorted. "Our marriage should have nothing to do with it. And you might stop thinking about yourself long enough to realize that I just might

48

have some talent for this sort of thing. It could open up an entire new life for me!"

"You've got talent all right," Kirk roared at the top of his voice. "A great talent for making a damned fool of yourself—and of me!"

Ronnie started to cry once again, running from the deck into the bedroom. Selfish, selfish, selfish, she assured herself. That's what's wrong with Kirk Ward. He's just plain selfish!

Kirk slammed down the back stairs, naked, and took a long walk down the deserted beach, thinking furiously.

Later, he returned to the beach house, and he and Ronnie clung to each other, until dawn streaks lightened the horizon.

But it wasn't as good as it had been.

Chapter VI

THE REST of Ronnie's first week was a whirl of excitement, new scenes, a new sense of importance and of living.

For Marty, it was a whirl of multitudinous detail; of grim fighting with her art department—with the photographer in charge of the color portraits of Ronnie—with the hairdresser, who insisted on trying to twist the lovely young socialite's soft waves into a monstrous beehive of teased, impossibly high-structured hair. Marty even fought with her pet faggot, Eric. The "gay" young makeup artist had indeed—as Marty had prophesied—fallen in love with Ronnie's face. But Marty screamed that he had taken leave of his senses when he began experimenting with wild eye-shadow, pale purple lips, green makeup beneath the cheekbones. Until Marty straightened him out, he lost track completely of her elegant simplicity.

Marty had come up with the idea of using Ronnie on radio commercials as well as in the other advertising media. She wasted no time, once the decision was made, and added a speech instructor to the already large crew with which she was surrounding her star. Not, Marty told Veronica, that she didn't have the loveliest of cultured voices, but for radio it was a distinct advantage to train your voice to a lower pitch to help eliminate any resentment from the listeners.

Ronnie was amused, but went along with everything Marty suggested. She was having the time of her life, she admitted to herself, and to Kirk every night when she came home tired but happy.

The commercials began to come down from the copy writers, finally reaching the mood Marty was demanding. Those accepted described the glories of Movie Starlet cosmetics, the appreciation and use of them by the fabulous Veronica Ward. Each word was a gem, set with polished care and sent forth with a sparkling message of hope for the poorer women of the world. To listen to those messages was to hear that every working woman in the world could—and would, with the help of Movie Starlet—become a goddess of love, a living testament to the magic of Marty's cosmetics.

Before the week was over, Ronnie was walking around in a trance, and Marty was understandably pleased at New York's about-face as the new copy and art layouts were received.

Friday was a hectic day for all concerned, and it was with relief that Ronnie left the offices for a two-day rest. She actually was looking forward to being with Kirk, she realized. It had been a long time since she'd known such anticipation.

That same Friday night Marty stayed on in her office after the rest of the hard-pushed "team" members had gone home. She knew that she was too keyed up to really rest. She had concentrated intensely on the new campaign, failing to pay heed to the warning symptoms of her body. The constant nearness of Ronnie, the many glimpses of her firm, white flesh in the fitting room, the thrill of touching her hair when the stupid hairdresser had finally returned it to its own soft, lovely style—all of these things had been pushed into the background. Now, Marty faced a lonely weekend of trying to keep them there. However, she vowed as she turned off the last lamp in her office and started out the doorway, that no matter how much she might hurt, she wasn't going to make the scene at The Song again. It always upset her. She still hadn't recuperated from the ugliness of that last affair. What was her name? Betty? She hardly remembered.

Marty had been home about fifteen minutes when the telephone rang. She'd mixed herself a Martini, which was failing to serve its purpose, and was preparing to shower. In fact, she had just stripped off her garter belt and nylons when the call came in.

She frowned in annoyance, crossed the room to the telephone (stopping on the way to grab the glass holding the remains of her now luke-warm Martini) and picked up the interfering instrument, almost angrily.

"Yes?"

"Marty?" It was a woman's voice. A voice that was rich, deep and caressing. A voice filled with promise.

At first Marty didn't recognize the speaker. Despite this, she felt a small tingling thrill race down her back.

"Yes. This is Marty."

The soft voice on the other end of the phone chuckled. "I wonder if you're feeling as I do?"

Still not recognizing the voice, but well keyed to the implications beneath its tone and words, Marty replied, "I don't know. How *are* you feeling?"

"You know, the 'Thank God it's Friday' kind of way."

"Dianne!"

The caller laughed again, throatily. "You are so right. And guess what Dianne has in mind?"

Marty didn't have to guess. When Dianne called, it could mean but one thing—she was once again ready to do a bit of "fence-jumping." Another thrill ran through Marty as she remembered just how accomplished Dianne was at this particular form of activity.

"No, tell me," Marty teased, hiding her own excited reaction.

"I can do much better than that," Dianne suggested. "Why don't I be over there in just a few minutes and *show* you? Unless, of course, you have something else on the calendar for this beautiful Friday night?"

"No, not really. I *was* expecting another call a little later on," she added, as a taunting afterthought. "But that one can wait. In fact, I'll make good and sure it *will* wait. So why don't you come on over? I'll be watching for you." She put down the receiver without hearing an answer. She knew what it would be. Thoughtfully she wondered, have I teased her enough? It would never do to let her know that she hit me at the best of all possible times—nor, she added honestly, that I probably need *her* tonight much more than she needs me. As she tossed down the dregs of her Martini, Marty suddenly remembered that it had been Dianne Van Lau who had arranged her meeting with Ronnie Ward. Shall I thank her for sending me that lovely little pigeon? Shall I tell her my plans?

Shaking her head, she strode purposefully toward the bathroom to take her shower. Better forget about Ronnie tonight, she warned herself. That's for later on. Right now it's Dianne who can give me my kind of loving. But beneath the needle jets of hot water, Marty continued to think about Ronnie Ward. She dreamed, as she soaped herself luxuriously, of the day when she could finally make her first move in the assault of that lovely hunk of plunder. She was quite sure she could arouse the girl to the point of surrender. As she turned the hot water down and gasped beneath the assault of the stinging cold spray, she thought of the swelling thighs and jutting breasts she'd glimpsed in the wardrobe room all week. She realized she'd never seen the color of the nipples, and found herself hoping they'd be pink.

She also felt her swelling appetite for sexual satisfaction, and hurriedly finished her shower, wishing that Dianne would arrive soon.

She heard the doorbell as she was toweling. Marty smiled to herself, ran a comb through her damp, tousled locks, tossed on a sheer nylon gown and ran to the door. Dianne, it was obvious immediately, was equally hungry.

She took one look at Marty, fresh from the shower, eyes gleaming with the excitement of her recent thoughts about another woman, and thrust herself through the doorway, slamming it quickly behind her. Reaching out, she pulled Marty to her in a frantically torrid embrace.

"My God, Marty," she exclaimed, "you smell so fresh, you look so absolutely clean. Oh, Marty, you're just adorable!" As she spoke, Dianne's hands were busy stroking Marty's damp hair, her soft cheek, and beginning to stray down her neck toward the velvet shoulders.

Marty laughed and pushed the excited woman from her. "Take it easy, Dianne. That can come a little later."

"But—"

"But, what?"

"You said you were expecting another call—later."

"If you'd just calm yourself down, you'd remember that I also said I'd make damned good and sure that the other call would wait its turn. On top of which, my lovely little switch-hitter, I told you to come over, that I'd be waiting. You don't think, do you—" and Marty whirled about in an oddly awkward imitation of a girl flirting with the newest male TV star, "that I'd have asked you over if I didn't have plans for you? What got you in this mood, anyway. Husband number eight not delivering?"

Dianne accepted both the flirtatious whirl, and the temporizing of her passions. She knew Marty. She knew Marty would have her way. She rummaged through her purse for a pack of cigarettes before she answered her question, however. "Frankly, darling," she said between puffs, "I actually think the poor bastard is a faggot! You know me—old 'sex-in-any-form'—and this boy can't make the grade! I'm desperate, darling, but *desperate!*"

Marty ran to her bedroom. "I'll be back in a flash. You know where the drinks are, dear. Make a pitcher of Martinis, but cold! And put some music on. I'll be back in a jiff!"

"It's good to know you'll be back in *something*, sweetie," Dianne called after her, "a flash or a jiff. I'll be waiting!"

Marty slipped into a hostess gown that revealed rather than concealed her lush figure. She had an idea for the evening, and she wanted to test it. She ran a brush carelessly through her hair, allowing it to adjust itself in soft waves. When she re-entered the living room, Dianne whistled.

"Darling, you look more femme than butch! If I didn't know better, I'd . . ."

Marty interrupted. "Perhaps I am, tonight. A little. Would you object?"

Dianne handed Marty a frosty Martini, licking her lips nervously. "I'm not sure. Not sure at all. I've never played it butch, you know. Never."

"There's a first time for everything."

"Yes," Dianne nodded. "There is, indeed. Which reminds me—how's Ronnie? Or, I should say, how are *you* and Ronnie?"

Marty smiled inwardly. This line of questioning was a little to obvious. "Mrs. Ward? She seems a rather nice person. I believe she can help the firm, particularly with her beauty and her social assets. Why do you ask?"

"You mean you haven't . . ."

"Don't be silly, darling." Marty's laugh tinkled. "I can't thank you enough for arranging the meeting with me. Remind me to send you a lifetime supply of my beauty aids."

"That slop?"

Dianne was not to know it until much later, but those words had changed her life, the life of Ronnie Ward, and most particularly, the life of Martha Browning.

Marty tossed her head, by way of reply, and indicated her need for another drink. But she wasn't thinking—at this point—about a one-night love affair, nor had she any particular need for another drink. This Movie Starlet thing—actually the first of such campaigns to the Amour company, and the first of any campaign in which Marty had invested her own preciously held money— was becoming a thing of a bête-noir. Her personal life was suffering. Under any other circumstance, she'd have gone on the make for a woman like Ronnie as soon as she saw her. She'd held back this time because of business. Her eyes narrowed as she watched the beautiful Dianne mix the drink.

How much, she wondered, does she hate Ronnie? And how much of her hatred is due to jealousy because she isn't, and never can be, that kind of a woman? She decided to test her theory. Marty wanted to know just what plans Dianne had in mind when she arranged for her own lover to meet a beautiful, lost lady.

She started her test by ignoring the subject.

"That slop," she said, accepting the drink, "as you might call it, is going to be sponsored by a good friend of yours. Mrs. Kirk Ward. And it's going to pay a helluva lot of bills for—well, for both of us." Marty took a sip of her drink as she watched for Dianne's reaction to the 'both of us' line. She was rewarded when she saw the woman wince.

"You've forgotten, Dianne, darling," and she moved closer to the other woman as she spoke, "*all* cosmetics come out of the same slop-pail. True, Amour has always gone the class-route. We—and I'm using the editorial 'we'—have always cost a great deal of money. My— and I do mean 'my'—new line isn't any step up the road as far as class is concerned. However—" and once more she studied her mistress-for-the-night, "your friend, Mrs. Ward, is going to make it look as though it is. But then, Dianne, I don't expect you to discuss my business affairs when you visit me. It's obvious you don't know too much about beauty aids. Or your husbands—ex-husbands, that is, wouldn't be numbered in the sevens, would they?"

Dianne's immediate reaction was one of anger, but then she caught the slow smile on Marty's face, and the slow, tantalizing crossing of her slender leg. The anger dissolved into the need of immediate forgetfulness—the need to prove she hadn't failed men as a woman. The desperate need to prove it was all their fault!

"*They* were husbands, weren't they, Dianne?" Marty continued her castigation of her victim. "And I'm not. You may be high on the male. You may continue marrying them. But I'm not a male. In fact, tonight, I feel like a damned well-endowed *female*."

Dianne poured herself another drink as she looked at Marty with confused emotions. For all the world, she thought to herself, she's acting like a femme. But she's always been my butch. Whenever I've wanted this kind of love, Marty's been my lover. She downed the drink quickly and poured another. Unable to keep her imagination away from their forthcoming affair, in which she seemed destined to play the unfamiliar role of "butch," Dianne sat beside Marty.

"Well," she said breathlessly, "here we are. Let's have another little drinkie while I appreciate your new-found femininity. Sort of give me a chance to lose any last minute inhibitions, huh?"

Marty laughed out loud. "You—Dianne. With inhibitions? Forgive me, baby, but I have to laugh."

"Laugh away. I do have one or two of those out-moded things left." Dianne poured two more drinks from the almost empty pitcher, and raised her glass in a toast. "Down to inhibitions. Up with Marty, the magnificent mistress!"

57

Marty accepted the toast, and smiled with a secret, inward sense of joy. She realized that she'd been right about the viciousness behind Dianne. She also determined, on the spot, that Dianne needed a large dose of meek humility. Making her be the butch tonight, when she so obviously was desperate to prove herself a femme, just might do the trick. At least she would give it a good try.

Marty lifted her glass to a toast for Dianne. "Up with me, you say. I say thank you. And—down with all clothing!"

Dianne's eyes widened with all of her mixed emotions. She placed her glass carefully upon the table, stood equally carefully upon her spike-heeled shoes. Then she stripped her pale blue frock from her body, almost tearing it in her anxiety. The expensive dress was followed quickly by her half-slip, bra and lace panties. Next went the shoes, nylons and garter belt. She stood, posed but not quite poised, before Marty, who sat drinking her in.

You must concede, Marty said to herself, that she has, despite her husbands and all of her dissipation, a beautiful, lovely, firm and succulent body. Marty allowed her gaze to wander over and around the charms of Dianne. Her eyes took in Dianne's swelling thighs, her proud, rose-tipped breasts, her flat, still soft stomach.

Marty sighed. She was beginning to wish she hadn't suggested this turnabout in their usual roles. Right at this point she wanted nothing more than to possess Dianne— rather than to be possessed by her. Putting the wish out of her mind and replacing it with the intrigue of her original plan, Marty zipped open the satin edged zipper on her hostess gown. She stepped out of it, wearing only her high heels and a smile of seductive triumph.

"Oh, oh," moaned Dianne, and she moved quickly to the other woman, taking her into her warm arms, pressing their bodies together. They were exactly the same height, and their breasts burned together as Dianne continued to encircle Marty's body with her demanding arms, probing the sweetness of her mouth with a questing tongue.

The two beautiful young women sank to the couch and remained as one while Dianne's fingers cunningly stroked and explored every inch of Marty's exquisite body. Strangely enough, although the switch in roles had been an idle, half-thought plan of revenge on Marty's part, she found herself enjoying the love-making—enjoying it far too much for her future peace of mind. Remember, she tried to tell herself between the gasps of passion she could no longer control, remember that you're Marty Browning, one hundred per cent butch. As she slipped into uncontrollable rapture she could only think how wonderful it was to be a femme—how sorry she'd never known this thrill before.

Dianne had been reticent to go along with Marty's idea, and had done so only because she knew that when a woman crossed Marty, she might well be thrown out without being satisfied. She, too, found herself strangely excited by the reversal of their sex roles. She couldn't refrain from the little moaning sighs she made as she kissed Marty's breasts, her shoulders, her stomach. . . .

Later, when both were pleasantly exhausted, they shared a cigarette. Dianne, still enjoying her role as butch, petted Marty and insisted that she lie still as *she* got up to mix more drinks. Dianne wasn't yet over her excitement, but Marty was another story. She felt drained, surfeited and strangely let down. She found her thoughts drifting back to Ronnie Ward, and as Dianne turned back toward the couch, Marty watched her with slitted eyes.

Dianne knelt and kissed Marty's thigh gently and handed her a drink. "Here," she said, rising to sit beside the lovely dyke, "Drink up, Marty. You know, we—you and I—have opened up a whole new world for ourselves. I never realized how much fun *you've* been having —all these years being the man in your woman's world. But, believe me, from now on I'm going to take turns with you. I might even—" and she turned to Marty, passion still flickering in her dark eyes, "take a shot at making another woman. But don't worry, honey," patting Marty's knee with a gesture of pure masculine condescension, "we'll get together again, real soon."

"You enjoyed it that much?" Marty was smug, ready to drop her small bomb.

"But of course, lover."

"Then I'll tell you something, lover," Marty had pulled away from the other woman, and her voice as well as her eyes had taken on a certain nastiness, "you can get yourself another playmate—if you can find another one who will keep her mouth shut!"

Dianne was staring at her in wide-eyed amazement.

"Don't look any kookier than you are. Big deal—you're *so* surprised you enjoyed being a butch. Look, Mrs. Dianne What's-your-name, don't you know after going through seven—almost eight—husbands that you aren't quite normal?" Marty's deliberately cheap words were spoken with biting coldness.

"Not normal?" Dianne's voice was rising to a shrill note. "I certainly *am* normal. I might like to party, but I'm no damned lesbian—which is more than you can say!" She started to rise from the couch and was stopped by an angry push of Marty's strong left hand.

"You certainly aren't a 'damned lesbian.' You're not good enough to be one of us. You might call it partying, but I've heard quite a few stories about some of your parties, baby. The leather boots, the whips, the satin cords, the whole bit! You're no les. You're a stinking pervert—not even as good as a sideshow freak. And I have neither the time nor the inclination to bother with either—a sideshow freak, or a pervert!"

Dianne was crimson with shame, anger and a sharp pain at the realization that Marty was probably closer to the truth than she knew. She made a half-hearted attempt to defend herself. "I've never . . ."

60

"Of course, you've 'never.' Only 'never' *what* is the question, no?" Marty was hot for the kill now. "Look, Dianne, I was in the mood for some light sexual companionship tonight. You gave it to me. Like a whore you gave it to me. For the free drinks, the sense of safety because I wouldn't expose *myself,* to tell stories on *you.* You can't even take care of your men, sweetie, so don't start messing around with women. *Me, I can take care of my broads!* And, for your information—" Marty moved in close, to make her point even more telling "—thanks to you, my next full-time femme is going to be Veronica Ward. You might have thought your little scheme went unnoticed. Don't worry, it didn't, but it's not going to work out your way. Because Ronnie's coming in a door that's locked for good to you. She's a real woman, Dianne, not a stupid, perverted, unsatisfactory switch-queen like you!"

Dianne stared at the woman in horror, as Marty turned her back and, striding across the room, threw open the door to the bath.

"Get out of this room. Get in there and get dressed, then get out of this house! And don't come back. The next time you want a woman—butch or femme—find yourself another girl. You're through here."

As the now-sobbing Dianne scooped up her clothing and ran toward the bathroom, Marty threw a final scathing remark into the wind behind her.

"You'd better not use any of the makeup. The only stuff in there is 'that slop' I make—and it's too rich for your skin!"

Dianne's answer was the slamming of the bathroom door.

Marty put on her robe slowly, poured another Martini from the fresh batch her recent "lover" had mixed, and laughed out loud when she heard the sound of retching coming from her bathroom.

Chapter VII

DAY AFTER DAY Ronnie seemed, to Kirk, to become more vivacious and gay. She was taking a deep interest in her career. She was also, obviously, working quite hard at it.

Marty—or "Miss Browning" as Ronnie still thought of her during the work-day—was highly appreciative of her interest and hidden talents. Or, so Kirk was led to believe. There were rumors, Ronnie told him, of an impending increase in salary. But, more important, Ronnie had remained "model" for a very short time. Becoming bored she had spent much of her free time in absorbing the more difficult aspects of the highly competitive advertising field. She was telling Kirk about her newly found knowledge this evening as they sat lazily sipping cocktails. Both of them, she thought with deep satisfaction, a bit tired from a "hard day at the office."

"It isn't the glamour, darling. And you, of all people, must know it isn't the money!" Ronnie explained intently. "It's just knowing that I can handle this sort of work, can understand and offer good thoughts and ideas. For example, what did I know about newspaper and magazine layouts a few weeks ago? Nothing! About coordination between copy, art, point-of-sale merchandising and sales force? Nothing! But during that short period of time I've learned a great deal. For the first time in my life I can realize the effort and thought that goes into a simple campaign to make a product desirable to the great god 'customer.' "

"You could have learned it from me," Kirk replied quietly. He was getting more than a little tired of seeing an exhausted Ronnie at the end of each of *his* exhausting days. He'd grown accustomed to coming home to a relaxed and beautiful wife, or to meeting the same radiant woman at a smart lounge for cocktails, then on to a good dinner on the Strip.

"Tomorrow," Ronnie bubbled on happily, failing to notice Kirk's mood, "I have an interview on tape with a public relations director for a non-competitive firm. An organization which is *very* big in the field of cleansing tissues. If we can get together we'll show their product in a bathroom shot, maybe even with a fast, almost subliminal C.U., and they'll pay a third of our nut for both film *and* time." She added modestly, "It was my idea."

Kirk said nothing, but scowled.

"Why darling, you look so—so 'scowly.' Don't you think it's a good idea?"

"Of course." Kirk's words were dripping with sarcasm. "Of course. It's a *very* good idea. It's just that this kind of crap is exactly the same kind of crap I have to listen to all day.

"I hope you don't mind my saying so, but I really don't particularly care to come home from ten or twelve hours of listening to it only to hear more of it from the luscious lips of my child bride. However, I apologize for the scowl." Kirk took a deep sip from his drink. "Go on, Ronnie. You were saying . . . ?"

"Kirk. Are you jealous because I'm successful? You are, I know. But why? Maybe because I'm earning more a week than you did when you first started." Ronnie took a gulp from her glass before continuing. "I didn't think you'd be chauvinistic, my darling."

"Goddamn it!" Kirk exploded. "Don't you dare take

refuse in that female bomb shelter of 'male chauvinism.' It all comes back to the fact that I've made a great deal of money. I also *have* a great deal of money. Furthermore, I expect to make a great deal more money. So, money we don't need. You're working for recognition and some sort of a warped kind of self-satisfaction— No! Wait!" He held up a hand to stifle her angry reply. "You just wait for me to finish. All I'm trying to tell you, Ronnie, is that you don't have to prove anything to anyone, except maybe yourself. Once you understand that, you'll have to admit the entire business of your working is a very selfish move on your part. Oh, I also happen to be feeble-minded enough to feel that if you didn't have to work when you were 'between' husbands, you sure as hell shouldn't join the slave labor corps when you're married to a millionaire. Can't you realize that our cook makes more than you do? Personally, I'm lonely for the wife who used to please me, entertain my friends, and run a fairly big household. What have I got? A wife who knocks herself out at less salary than my cook, than my *secretary*, by God, all to show that she can 'prove' herself! Well, in my book you've proved yourself, all right. Proved yourself to be a featherheaded little idiot who is willing to see her marriage go on the rocks, who is willing to embarrass her husband just to satisfy some juvenile need for 'expression,' whatever the hell that's supposed to mean. And another thing— Oh, what's the use," he concluded, still angry as he saw the cold, impassive look on her face that meant his message wasn't getting through.

Ronnie had kicked off a pump before this tirade and had been thoughtfully massaging her foot while she listened. She slid her shoe back on and went to the bar to pour herself another drink. Kirk noted she'd been drinking a little more every day since the new job had started, and he wasn't very happy about it. She came back, drink in hand, and looked at him thoughtfully.

"Kirk, are you issuing an ultimatum? 'Either-or' sort of thing?"

Kirk stubbed out his cigarette and sat forward on the sofa. Here was a situation he confronted several times a week, and he knew all the answers.

"Why do you ask that?"

"I'll tell you why—if you think you can tell *me* to quit this position 'or else,' you've got another think coming. I'll be packed and out of here so fast—"

Kirk nodded gently. Pavlov's dogs. A conditioned reflex. "It seems to me, Ronnie, that *you* just issued the ultimatum. I stated, loudly enough, that I'm not happy with the way things are. I didn't threaten you with anything. Aren't you being a little quick on the trigger?"

"Oh, Kirk, I . . . well, this is *important* to me. Can you understand? I need to establish some sort of identity for myself." She began to cry.

Kirk pulled her down to his lap and kissed her forehead tenderly. "Sure, baby. Sure, I know. But don't ever threaten to leave your old husband. You know I couldn't live without you. Everything I've done, I've done for you. I wanted you to be proud of me, of being Mrs. Kirk Ward. Prouder than you ever could have been married to that —that—"

"Charles? Whatever brought him into your mind, dear? I haven't seen Charles Hyton since the day we got our divorce, and you know it."

"Well, baby, like it or not, Charles is the reason I haven't put my foot down harder on this deal of yours. You told me once that he was ambitious. Wealthy, but ambitious. So greedy for money he even hinted he wouldn't be too awfully upset if you slept with a business rival so that he could dig up a little scandal and apply the pressure. I made up my mind when we were married that I wouldn't bring my job home with me. All I asked was that you be an understanding, lovely wife. Well, you have been. Up until now. I think you will be again, as soon as you get this 'identification' bug out of your system. So, I guess I can afford to be patient."

She pressed a damp cheek to his. "Sweetheart, I promise I won't bring my job home with me anymore."

"Nonsense. Tell me all about it at the end of each day. It might do you some good. Maybe I can help you from time to time. I have a *little* experience with advertising and publicity, you know."

He kissed Ronnie soundly on the lips, patted her sleek thigh. "Now let's go out to the kitchen and see what's left to eat on cook's day off."

And so the days passed. And the nights. Despite himself, Kirk wasn't able to abandon his body to the sort of ecstatic lovemaking that had marked their many nights together. It felt sort of—well, indecent, somehow, to spend your emotions on a woman who, instead of following the act of love with words of endearment, would light a cigarette and say: "Kirk, remember the double-page we were going to run in black and white in the magazine? I think I swung the budget up so that we can hit in color. Don't you think that would be much more effective?"

Kirk couldn't bring himself to ask Ronnie for a little more affection, and finally he almost stopped feeling passion altogether. Might as well make love to an advertising agency! He felt his manhood, even his vigor being undermined and didn't know what to do about it.

On the reverse side of the coin, Ronnie, still blithely certain that there would be a closer *rapport* now that she could knowledgeably speak Kirk's language, became bitter and frustrated at his coolness.

So two people, very much in love with each other, found themselves drifting apart. Just a little, perhaps, but drifting. Ronnie's pride prevented her from attempting a reconciliation, while Kirk's bafflement prevented him from even acknowledging that there was a rift. Kirk and Ronnie both rather circumspectly avoided the subject of sex, which was becoming not only unsatisfactory but almost non-existent in their relationship.

Kirk had studiously avoided any queries into his wife's business life, and she had just as studiously tried to avoid any further mention of it. Yet there was a need on both sides, so that when Miss Bradley informed Kirk that his wife had called and said she'd be delayed this evening and would he mind picking her up at her office "about six-ish," Kirk rather looked forward to seeing the inner workings of this emporium of packaged beauty. Ronnie was confident, on the other hand, that he'd be impressed with what he did see.

In the advertising offices of "Movie Starlet," Marty took off her glasses and sat back in her chair, rubbing the pink marks on her patrician nose. "When you're finished with that last paragraph, just drop the acetate over it and let the damned thing lay until morning, Ronnie."

Ronnie nodded. She was terribly impressed and terribly excited. This was the kickoff for the major campaign, the do or die, all-out effort that would make or break the new product aimed at the masses. She laid the sheet of acetate back gently.

"Miss Browning, I—"

"Marty."

"Yes. Marty, I can't tell you how much faith I have in this campaign, or what a wonderful job you've done!"

Marty lit a pair of cigarettes, handed one to Ronnie. "Yes," she said, dryly, "I suppose you are excited. The thing is, will the consuming female, with her dollar bill clutched in her dishwater reddened paw, will that female think so, too? Will they believe all this crap about 'Movie Starlet' making them look as glamorous as a motion picture actress or as glamorous as . . . well, *you*? By the way, did you see the rushes the studio delivered this morning on your introduction to the series?"

"Honestly," Ronnie confessed, perching on the edge of the table beside Marty, "I never felt so foolish, so . . .

well, *dumb* in my life. And you said you were going to dub in the voice, but you used mine. Why?"

Marty chuckled, patted one of Ronnie's shapely thighs so well-evidenced under her tight skirt. "Why improve on perfection? Listen, your voice is as perfect for the whole bit as your face or your figure. My God, where did you get such a complexion? Smooth as a baby's backside."

"I hate to admit this, Marty—I don't use cosmetics. No lotions or creams. I get up in the morning, wash my face with soap and water. I put on a little lipstick. Nothing else. Oh, when I go home, I shower. If we're going out, I might use a touch of eyeshadow. Nothing else. I've tried all sorts of makeup, and my skin feels as if it can't breathe."

Marty made a mock-groan. "Good God, I'm nurturing the A-bomb in my bosom. Listen, don't tell a soul. Remember, you're a 'Movie Starlet' girl!"

"Of course."

They sat in companionable silence, idly swinging their legs.

"What are you looking at?"

Marty almost blushed. "Your legs. You have very lovely legs. It gave me a germ of an idea. Maybe we can set up a tie-in with a stocking manufacturer. You know, send in the labels from so many 'Movie Starlet' jugs and fifty cents for a pair of sheer nylons. Hey, how would your hubby go for your showing a little cheesecake on the tube?"

"Leg art?"

"Sure. And you could do it. Why fool around blowing money on another model when we've already got you working on salary? Look at the money we could save on residuals alone! Here, let me show you. Not too much leg, you know. Just a bit above the knee. Then we'll have some oily-voiced bastard ask the grandma's out in Pasadena how they'd like to have *their* legs so smooth, so chic, so glamorous? I tell you, it's a natural. Here, swing your legs up on the table. That's right. Now hoist the dress just a *little*."

She stepped back, framing the picture with her hands.

"Wait, that's not a natural position." She went to Marty slid her around a bit, urged one knee crossed a bit more, straightened a stocking seam, stepped back muttering to herself, then came up and raised the skirt just a bit higher.

"Good evening," said a man's voice gravely from behind them. It was Kirk, and his face showed neither pleasure nor displeasure. He was carefully noncommittal.

Marty whirled, looked. "Who are you?"

"I'm your . . . er . . . model's husband." It was a statement, nothing more, beyond a slight inflection that might not have been intended.

Ronnie was a bit dismayed, although she couldn't figure out the reason. "We were just trying a pose for a stocking commercial," she offered.

"Your wife has lovely legs," Marty volunteered.

"I'm sure you find them so. I've always thought so myself, although I have the *purely* masculine viewpoint. Stocking commercial, eh? I thought this was a cosmetics firm?"

Marty flushed. The bastard was on to her, all right. "In advertising, Mr. Ward, we do many things. Many things."

He raised a sardonic eyebrow. "I'm sure you do. Some of them must be highly entertaining. And yet, I can see where there would be a few problems, as well."

This brief contest of wits was all above Ronnie. She listened but didn't understand. She hopped off the table, ran to Kirk and kissed him. He stared, rock-like over her shoulder squarely into Marty's eyes. She, too, was over her initial embarrassment and returned his glare. It was to be open war. Good enough.

Ronnie spoke up. "Ready to go, darling? Did you get my message? Well, of course you did or you wouldn't be here. Marty, would you care to join us somewhere for cocktails?"

"No thanks, dear," Marty spoke slowly, emphasizing the 'dear,' "I've got a few more hours work. Nice to have met you, Mr. Ward."

Kirk bowed his head. He was, he knew, looking at a formidable challenger. "Nice to have met you, too, Miss . . . ah . . ."

"Browning. Marty Browning."

"Indeed. I'll remember that." Ronnie preceded him out the door. He turned. "Goodnight—*Martin*."

Marty sneered, and it changed her face.

Ronnie chattered excitedly about the new campaign all the way to the car, but Kirk had nothing to say. He headed straight toward home.

"Aren't we going to stop off somewhere?"

"We'll have cocktails—and a long talk—at home."

"Oh, I get it, my boy is hungry. Well, cook promised to have nice prime ribs for you tonight. Good." She snuggled back in her seat, humming contentedly. Things were working out beautifully.

Things didn't, though.

When they pulled up in the drive, Kirk muttered something reasonably obscene at the sight of cook's new Cadillac. Ordinarily the sight amused him—it was a year newer than his own—but it wasn't funny tonight.

He shut off the ignition, switched off the lights, came around and opened Ronnie's door. She got out quietly enough. "Something go wrong at the office today?"

"Not at my *office*. Let's go in."

Kirk went straight to the kitchen and told the cook to go home. The maid came in only three days a week and today was her day off, which was just as well. She was ordinarily impertinent, and Kirk was in no mood for impertinence. He stayed in the kitchen until cook had gone out the back door.

Taking a deep breath, he entered the living room.

Ronnie had thrown herself carelessly down on the sofa. The sight of a white thigh carelessly revealed above a

70

sheer stocking top enraged him. It looked too sickeningly like the scene that had greeted his eyes as he'd walked in, unannounced, at the "Movie Starlet" office.

"Will you kindly pull down your dress!" he bellowed, pushed beyond endurance.

Ronnie raised astonished eyes from the evening newspaper. "Don't you like my legs? Marty says I have lovely legs, better than a professional model."

"I'll bet she does! Well, she's welcome to whatever fun she may have had, but she's seen the last of you. I hope she had a hell of a good look at your legs. I forbid you to go back to that damned bull-dyke. You want a job, fine, I'll get you a job. Pays more money, too!"

Ronnie heard only one word. *"Bull-dyke?"*

Kirk snorted in disgust. "Are you blind? Look at her! One look would tell you what she is, if you weren't blinded by this so-called 'glorious opportunity' to establish your identity. Christ, if I hadn't walked in when I did, she'd have had your dress up around your shoulders!"

"I've never heard anything so ridiculous in my life. She's a hard-working woman in a man's world. I told you that you were a male chauvinist and you are! Marty's a dear friend and a fine executive, and that's all she is. I think you owe me an apology!"

"Don't hold your breath waiting for it, kid. You wanted ultimatums in the past—I'll give you an ultimatum. Shake that stinking lesbian, or move into the guest room until I can get a good private detective on this thing. It shouldn't be much trouble to get the evidence. In fact, if I'd had a camera with me tonight when I walked into your office, I'd *have* all the evidence I need!"

"Evidence?" Ronnie was in tears. "Evidence for what? A divorce?"

Kirk went to the bar, poured himself a double, held it up critically to the light, added another shot for good measure and tossed it down in one angry motion.

71

"For a divorce," he agreed. "You named it right. For a divorce."

He, rather than Ronnie, slept in the guest room that night. He slept in an alcoholic stupor.

Ronnie didn't sleep at all, but lay staring dry-eyed at the ceiling.

Chapter VIII

THREE MORNINGS LATER, Ronnie left for the "Movie Starlet" offices, eyes burning from another sleepless night, a night spent listening to the sounds of her husband stumbling around the house, opening beer cans and bottles, blasting the stereo to all hours of the night, and finally falling asleep in a drunken stupor, and wherever he might happen to land.

She glanced over her shoulder as she walked out the wide glass entrance to her once loved home, and saw Kirk huddled miserably on one of the smaller couches in the nook beneath her curving stairway. A small twinge of empathy pinched her, only to be replaced by a stronger sense of the wrong Kirk had been doing—to both of them. She tried to put him out of her mind as she walked wearily toward the white T-Bird and took off down the driveway.

Kirk had been in a state of semi-consciousness throughout the night. His wife's hesitation at the doorway managed to seep through his alcoholic daze about twenty minutes after she had left. Sick as he was, he had a vague realization that he'd probably missed a good chance of making up with her. He pulled himself up from the small couch, stumbled toward the downstairs bathroom and was sick. He had done so every morning since the night he'd told Ronnie he wanted a divorce.

Miss Bradley was all but in tears when he left his office early that afternoon. Something awful was going to happen. Every instinct told her this, and she tried desperately to convey her thoughts and fears to her beloved boss.

It didn't work. Kirk left, compounding his felony with a remorseful lie as he noticed the tic in Miss Bradley's eyes about to give way to tears. "I'll be back later. And I'll call in from time to time. But I don't know where you can reach me between calls because, quite frankly, Miss Bradley, I don't know where I'll be." He gave her a wry smile which served only to tear her heart a little bit more.

By four o'clock that afternoon, Kirk was once again on his way to a heavy hangover. He'd spent most of his time going from bar to bar, having one—at the most two—in each spot. He was tempted to head for Malibu and The Key, but he remembered too well the disastrous ending to his last day with Johnny O'Shea. And he couldn't quite face the sight of the beach house and all the beautiful memories it held of Ronnie.

In an effort to get as far away as he could from anything he had shared with his wife, he headed for Hollywood and Vine. The Mecca of Midwestern tourists, and a spot to which no true Californian will venture except in extreme circumstances. He stood idly in front of the drugstore which was the glamourous southeastern corner of the famous intersection. He watched the garishly-clad tourists as they aimed their cameras at the street sign, trying in vain to find a glamourous angle from which to shoot. It wasn't much to offer them, really, Kirk thought to himself. They could pick the drugstore, a department store of no particular reputation, a coffee shop or an airline ticket office.

Hollywood and Vine!

Kirk walked down Vine Street about half a block until he spotted a neon sign which read simply "Bar— Whis-

74

key and Beer." The simplicity of it appealed to his mood so he walked in. He was momentarily blinded by the dimness of the place as compared with the brilliant California sunshine he'd just left. As he stood just inside the doorway, waiting for his eyes to adjust, he heard his name called in loud, positive tones. My God, was his first reaction. Who do I know who would possibly be in a place like this at four o'clock in the afternoon?

It was Dianne Van Lau.

And Dianne was on her umpteenth Martini—knowing only enough to stay away from her usual hangouts—having enough hope and faith in the human race to look for another patsy in this, for her, out-of-the-way spot. As she'd seen Kirk come in the door, Dianne's built-in bitchiness had told her she was about to have the chance of a lifetime in getting back at the envied Ronnie Ward. Another moment of study gave Dianne still more insight, and the very strong feeling that Marty Browning had more than a little to do with Kirk Ward's presence, half-drunk, in a Hollywood joint at four o'clock. Dianne decided to go for broke, and as she made her decision she let out a war whoop, summoning Kirk to her side.

"Kirk! Darling!" She was off the bar stool and, by some inexplicably rapid mode of movement, beside him before he'd actually adjusted his sights to the center of the attack. "You're waiting for Ronnie, I'm sure—" Both she and Kirk knew she was lying. She knew why. Kirk didn't. He was man enough in the woman jungle to be lost in the traps Dianne could set out—"But such an odd place to see either of you. Come, buy me a drink. We'll wait together."

Kirk had no choice. He motioned to the lanky, blonde bartender to give Dianne a drink and spoke his own order aloud. When she heard the "double Scotch, on the rocks" Dianne felt a small but clearly announced triumph. Kirk never drank Scotch. Something was wrong—real wrong. Dianne moved her stool slightly closer to Kirk's, as she played her game by ear.

"I hope, darling Kirk," she caressed his hand in a poor imitation of fond friendliness, "that your meeting your—well—your wife *here* doesn't mean it's going to be a showdown?"

Kirk, barely listening to Dianne, did hear the last words.

"Showdown? What kind of a showdown, Dianne? Don't tell me you're on one of those moody binges of yours again."

As she started to protest, he added, "Ronnie's told me about them. You hate the world, yourself and all you've done in the way of sinning. But, as Ronnie explained, you hate everyone else that knows you because they can't do the same—or, rather, because they haven't done the same things! Really, Dianne, I'm not in the mood for a mood tonight."

Dianne smiled inwardly. If anything, this Kirk Ward was more in a mood than he'd ever been. And if she knew her men (after eight husbands, twenty times more lovers and the women she'd known, who wouldn't know a simple man like this), he was lying in his teeth.

"Oh, come off it, Kirk. I know you and Ronnie. You both know me." Her Martinis were showing—badly— "I've shacked up with enough people at Malibu—at *your* beach house. If you don't know me, you're some kind of a kook or something. But let's be honest, baby. If you think *you're* surprised, how the hell do you think I felt when *I* found out about Ronnie?"

Kirk felt the tightening of his nerves, almost to the point of strangulation. Dianne's words hit him first in his mind—it promptly refused to accept them. Then they hit his heart, and he knew the coldest fear he'd ever known. Slowly they crept through his maleness—his masculinity —his body and his soul. He tried to use his brain. It was all a big thing. He was making something out of the fights he'd had, and the words of a stupid, amoral and very drunken woman. She couldn't mean what his every instinct told him she meant. He'd ignore her. That was the best way he could think of to shut her up. He ignored her for approximately two minutes. He had to know the truth. So, he made the biggest mistake of his life. He asked for the truth from a congenital liar—and a woman who hated his wife.

Dianne purred once again as the question hit his lips. Tell this chick she didn't know the right time to swing; she was just about to top both Clay and Liston for taking advantage of the biggest set-up either had ever seen.

"Just what," Kirk asked, "do you think you've found out about Ronnie? Just what do you think could bring us to a place such as this for a showdown? And just what are you, Mrs. Van Lau, doing here in the afternoon—and if I might be so bold—with more than the ordinary number of Martinis beneath that ever-so-slim belt of yours?"

She laughed to herself, savoring the moment. Tilted eyes dared Kirk to defy her, dared him to press her, dared him not to wait for her answer. And, along with the other provocations, dared him to buy her another drink. He got the last message first.

Dianne nodded, and even the nod didn't move the tilted, questioning, defiant eyes. Kirk sat still, growing coldly sober as each minute passed. He had, he felt, degraded himself enough by asking the first questions. He wasn't about to reiterate.

"I know about Ronnie and Marty Browning," Dianne replied, in a sudden, sober statement.

Kirk felt as though he were drowning. Ronnie and Marty? Oh, sure, he'd made the same accusation, but it had been made because he knew just how naive Ronnie was—because he'd spotted Marty as a bull-dyke from the moment he'd met her. His accusation hadn't really been an accusation, but a warning. But—and the cold crept over him again—almost like dying—if someone like Dianne had heard, or seen this relationship—what if, as Dianne had inferred, their love was a matter of common knowledge? Oh, God. Kirk could barely refrain from sobbing. He had to answer this bitch. He had to deny this lie.

Dianne felt one faint pang of remorse as she watched the emotions sweeping over Kirk's face. It was gone before she had recognized it for what it was. She moved in to kick Kirk while she had him down.

"The whole damned town knows about Ronnie and her lesbian lover, Kirk. I even thought of trying to talk her out of it, but you know how close-mouthed your *wife* can be when she wants to."

"You don't know what you're saying." Even to Kirk's ears, his voice sounded weak and his words ineffectual.

"You're not going to deny it! You can't think you could get away with that act on me!" Dianne leaned closer to Kirk, staring at him coldly, a mask of pseudo-friendship barely covering her hatred.

"But, Kirk. You didn't know. Oh my God!" Dianne began to laugh shrilly. "You're the husband—the one that's always the last one to know. I'm sorry, Kirk. Truly, I'm sorry." Dianne kept on laughing as she spoke. Kirk couldn't bring himself to look at her.

"I'm the last to know what, Dianne? Some wild, perverted lie about my wife? I thought you were her friend. Thank you for setting me straight on the matter." Kirk turned from Dianne and gave the interested bartender a signal for another drink. One. He was quite obviously ignoring Dianne's empty glass. She, in turn, refused to be ignored and gave the bartender a signal to fill it up. Kirk, mad though he was, had too much inbred gentility to refuse the check when the rattled bartender handed it to him.

"Please, Kirk. I know you're angry and hurt, but don't take it out on me. I might not be the most moral woman in the world, but there is a point where I draw the line. Rapping a friend is one of them." Dianne was amazed at the sincere ring of her words. She was also most pleased at their obvious effect upon Kirk. He looked physically ill.

He was physically ill. He looked into the mirror behind

the bar and saw not himself but the reflection of Marty and Ronnie as they'd been when he walked unexpectedly into their office. He tore his gaze away from the mirror in a conscious effort to refrain from screaming at the sight.

"Kirk." Dianne's hand touched his arm softly. "Please don't look like that, Kirk. You can't know how you're making me feel—how desperately sorry I am that I was the one to spill the ugly story to you."

"It's a lie, you know," Kirk muttered, almost beneath his breath.

Dianne heard the words. "I only wish it was, Kirk. I honestly wish I could believe it was a lie."

"Why can't you?"

"I told you I tried to talk to Ronnie about it."

"Yes?"

"She is, as you know, a very reticent woman. Unfortunately, her girl friend isn't."

"What do you mean, Dianne?"

"I mean I talked to Marty Browning."

Try though he might, Kirk couldn't withhold the next question. "What did she have to say about the stories?"

"Are you sure you want to hear it?"

For a short second, Kirk's native good sense and intelligence asserted themselves. He laughed shortly and replied, "You haven't given me much of a choice in the matter, have you, Dianne?"

She ignored the question, sipping her drink slowly as she chose just the right words to convince him. "Among many other interesting tid-bits, Miss Browning informed me that she could take care of her broads—that *I* wasn't good enough to be a lesbian—something about Mrs. Veronica Ward being a full time femme, and, as I recall, and this is an exact quote *'she's a real woman, Dianne, not just an unsatisfactory switch-queen like you.'* Is that enough, Kirk, or shall I try to drag some more of the conversation up from the dregs of my memory?"

Kirk stood up and walked rapidly toward the entrance. He didn't say good-by to Dianne.

He didn't say good-by to Ronnie either. He drove home, packed his clothes and called the Beverly Hills for a bungalow reservation—on a per-month basis. In the note he left for Ronnie he didn't tell her where he'd be staying. He didn't mention his meeting with Dianne. He didn't even mention Marty Browning—by name. He merely wrote: *"Next time you want a new lover, get rid of the old one first. I'm taking care of that little chore for you this time. Hope the new one will be as thoughtful when the time comes."*

He signed it simply "K."

Chapter IX

KIRK'S NOTE was brutal, perhaps, but certainly to the point. So much so that Ronnie sat staring blankly at the wall, too shocked to place one thought before the other, and arrive at a logical conclusion.

This *couldn't* be happening to her. She went to the kitchen, tasted the tuna casserole that the cook had thoughtfully prepared, shuddering at the taste, although it was ordinarily one of her favorite foods. She went back to the living room, poured a stiff shot of Scotch, drank part of it, wandered into the downstairs bath, flicked on the light and looked at herself in the mirror. Maybe Kirk had a younger, more beautiful woman. She critically examined her face. Still youthful, still firm, still no need for makeup.

She felt numb, almost emotionless. She knew that shortly—in a few moments, or an hour, or tomorrow, this false serenity would collapse and that she'd then be a quivering mass of humanity, helpless to retaliate against Kirk's scorn, his loathing. For *what?*

What had she done? She hadn't cheated on Kirk once during their married life, although God knows she'd had more than a fair share of opportunities—and propositions. She thought, with grim amusement, that Kirk would indeed be surprised if he were to know about some of them and their source—some of Kirk's closest "friends."

She tossed off the remainder of her drink. All right, the hell with him. She could get along very nicely without him. Money was no problem. She had more than enough in her own right to support her in comfort. And her position promised great things.

Where was Kirk?

She picked up the note, read it again. He gave no hint as to his destination or where he could be reached. Selfish, selfish, that's what he was! You think you're grieving, she told herself, but you're not. You're not—it's just that he's touched your pride. The woman scorned. Ha! Forget it. Forget him. "New lover," indeed. He was the one with a new lover, if anyone was. You don't need him, you can stand on your own two beautifully-proportioned legs . . . *wait a minute!*

Could it be that time he'd walked in as she and Marty were sort of rehearsing a shot for the television cameras, after office hours? No, she shook her head, hardly that. Oh, he'd been angry enough, all right, and had called Marty a "bull-dyke," but that had only been male chauvinism. Men didn't like to see women with really important executive positions. Besides, he'd been a lamb ever since, although not very demanding sexually. Perhaps that was it—perhaps the separate rooms had finally got to him!

Oh, he'd be back, no doubt of it. Just give him an hour or so to think it over, a few drinks to cool him down. She hummed a little song as she went to the bar, refilling her glass of Scotch. This time she added an ice cube, deliberately trying to close her mind to the note. Ignore it and it'll go away, she argued with herself. Think about tomorrow's work schedule. Busy, busy. Think busy. Fittings tomorrow. For a moment she allowed her mind to run pleasurably over the excitement she always got from the fittings. The pins and the little murmurs of admiration from the dressmaker and the wardrobe people.

Where was Kirk?

She took a gulp of her Scotch. Tears started from her eyes. She walked slowly back to the huge circular sofa. *She and Kirk had made love on it the day it had been delivered; got to test these things, he'd said.* She sank down, lost again in despondency. Well, old gal, cheer up. That telephone's going to ring. She watched it, waiting for it to ring. It looked like an ivory-colored, evil and malevolent monster squatting there.

"Ring, damn you, *ring!*" she commanded, aloud. Her voice sounded strangely lonesome in the big, empty house. Is this how a ghost feels? She took another sip from her drink, coughed. Where were the cigarettes? On the table, next to the telephone. The rug stretched endlessly before her. She walked, all sense of time and distance held in reserve for some future, unknown, unperceivable occasion. She kicked off her pumps, and carefully, still holding her unfinished drink, made her way to the table. Don't look at the telephone and it will ring. A watched pot never boils. She took the cigarette package with her to the bar and carefully poured herself a topper. The tears started again.

Where was Kirk?

She put a hand to her mouth. It was a joke, that's what it was. Kirk had probably come home half-snockered, placed the note where she couldn't fail to see it and gone up to the guest room to sleep it off. Sure. Hell yes, that had to be it. She felt better. She took another sip from her drink and then carefully lit a cigarette. Really, she told herself, Kirk has an absolutely childish sense of humor. My God, he must know how frightened I'd get to walk into a scene like this. She opened her purse, took out a tissue and dabbed at her eyes. I probably look a solid fright, but he's too drunk to notice anyway, so let's get the show on the road. We've both been a bit too stiff-necked, saying cutting things to each other. If that man only knew how very, very much I love him. She finished her drink, giggled and decided to surprise Kirk.

She went softly up the steps, not turning on the hall light, and softly opened the door of the guest room.

I'll just crawl right in there with him, and when he wakes up we'll make love. I'll do any damn thing he wants. I'll even quit that stupid job. I love that boy, chauvinism and all! She turned on the lights. The bed was empty, unruffled.

A little chill ran down her back.

Aha! He's gone to our *bedroom. That's it. He's in our own bed, bless his heart!* She ran in stockinged feet down the hall. Into their room. Lights on—nothing. No one.

The bathroom! Oh, dear God, don't let it be the . . . she touched the knob, afraid to open it, afraid of what she might find inside. Would Kirk have been driven so far that he might have— Slowly, holding her breath, she turned the knob, pulling the reluctant door toward her. Dark. Well it might be. With a shuddering breath she turned on the light. She exhaled with a combination of relief and fear.

Kirk wasn't in the house, that much was clear. How dare he put her through such fear, such anxiety? She was all the way back down the stairs and mixing yet another drink when the awareness came.

She was alone.

The friendly old house was suddenly an ogre's den. Now there was no silence. Noises, unheard before, suddenly became loud. She wondered if the whiskey might be sharpening her preceptions, but of course that was nonsense. She heard a "drip" of water somewhere in the house. And an ominous creaking just outside the large french windows off the living room. She scurried around, turned on all the lights. There, that was better. She had another drink of Scotch, her eyes darting nervously

84

around the room. If you looked quickly enough, you could *almost* see *something* duck back around the corner of a door, under a drape, behind a piece of furniture. She shuddered. It had been a delicious fear, she remembered, during her childhood. She realized she was on the brink of hysteria. She drank quickly, a little of the Scotch trickling down her chin. She wiped at it with the back of her hand in a curiously childlike gesture.

Shortly, she fell asleep. An unhappy, troubled sleep, from which she half-woke from time to time. Her arm was wet the last time, and she realized that she'd been snoring and that the snoring had caused her to come sharply awake. She whimpered in her sleep.

Next morning, Marty was called, in her office. It was Ronnie, and Ronnie wasn't coming to work. Not that day, anyway.

"I'm ill," Ronnie said. "I don't want to ruin our schedule, especially at this stage of the game, but I'm just too ill, too exhausted to come in."

"I understand," Marty told her. "It's all right, baby. I'll cover for you in case things get a little sticky." She had a sudden hunch. "Kirk?"

Ronnie laughed a little too hysterically. "Kirk? Whatever gave you that . . . yes, it's Kirk. Marty, he didn't come home all night. And he left me a nasty note. Not," she hurried on, "that the note is important. I just hope he's all right."

Marty smiled grimly. "That's a man for you, every time. I'm sure he's okay. So listen, baby, you get some rest. Maybe this afternoon, huh? And if there's anything I can do—well, just call, right?"

Ronnie mumbled a thanks, and Marty put down the telephone, thoughtfully. So Kirk suspected. Good!

She went to the water cooler, sipping thoughtfully. No use kidding, she was really in love with her, hung up on Ronnie.

A hell of a note.

For Marty, the day passed slowly, so slowly she thought she'd scream from pure frustration.

I could go to her, she thought, and comfort her. And hold her and caress her. But that wasn't the same, that wasn't what she wanted, really. No, Marty wanted Ronnie to come to *her,* to need the comfort and solace she'd never find with a man. Thought turned to desire, desire to lust.

Marty left her office, the office of "Movie Starlet" early that day, went home and almost without thinking changed into her "butch" outfit: jeans, boots, leather jacket. Excitement was stirring her loins as she drove to "The Song" club. It was a busy afternoon and evening there. Marty shopped but didn't buy. Quite a few "femmes," knowing who Marty was, knowing her bankroll, made obvious overtures, passes which Marty would have picked up in other days. Somehow, Ronnie's sweet face interposed itself, and Marty shook off all the more-than-willing aspirants for a bed partnership. Damn! she thought, I'm going nuts!

Gail, for example. Gail was a femme, but an independent one. She had no steady "butch," playing the field instead. Gail was a willowy blonde with high, full bosom, dedicated to the lesbian relationship (rumor had it that she'd never known a man) and choosy with her favors. Marty had had eyes for Gail for many a moon, but hadn't been able to make the scene for a one-night stand. Tonight, Gail was not only approachable, but anxious.

"Hey," she murmured, taking the stool next to Marty, "you're all dyked out tonight! I bet you're in the mood, sugar."

Marty grunted. "Have a drink."

Gail laughed. "Sweet daddy, I *got* a drink. Listen," she breathed excitingly into Marty's ear, "you got eyes for me, haven't you? I'll tell you what—tonight's the night!" Her eyes blurred a little. She wet her lips suggestively. "Let's go to your house, sugar. I'll show you some things you've never seen before."

Marty stubbornly kept her head down, eyes focused on her drink. Gail giggled, leaned over and whispered obscenities into Marty's ear, sweet obscenities that a week ago would have caused Marty's blood pressure to leap. She bit Marty's ear lobe, and Marty backhanded her right off the bar stool. A gasp went up from the other patrons of The Song. Marty tossed a bill on the bar and walked rapidly to the exit. It wasn't until she hit the open air that the tears came. She sat for a long time behind the wheel of her car, crying in long, gasping sobs. Until now, it had been for kicks. Until now, it had been revenge on her mother and father, the father who'd always wanted a boy. Until now it had been a way of life, nothing for the general public, that big eighty-five per cent to know about.

But now—it was love. Love, sacred or profane. Love for Ronnie, love *with* Ronnie. Ronnie, innocent, straight, distressed because her *husband,* for God's sake, had stayed out all night!

Marty started the car, drove home unseeing. Had there been a careless driver coming in the opposite direction, there could have been a disastrous accident, because Marty couldn't even remember how she got back to her comfortable, yet strangely lonely apartment, high above The Strip.

Once home, she threw the "butch" garb into a closet with great self-disgust. Such a childish thing, she told herself. Who needs it? Stupid. Sick.

She went to the bathroom, combed her hair into a feminine style and slipped into a frilly nightgown. She went to bed early, drinking nothing. She lay there, staring at the ceiling, full of disgust for herself and for the world that made it impossible for her to have an open relationship with Ronnie, or at least to allow her to compete openly for Ronnie's charms, her wit, her vivacity. God damn all men! she thought, savagely, trying vainly to stifle her self-disgust, her self-pity.

The telephone rang.

It was Ronnie. She tried to keep the exaltation out of her voice as she answered.

"Yes, Ronnie?" Oh, let it be tonight!

"I . . . I can't stay by myself any longer, Marty. Kirk hasn't called or come home. I have to talk to someone. I'm going crazy. Please, may I come over and talk things over with you? I know it's a terrible imposition, you probably have plans for the night, but if I don't talk to someone, have *some* human contact, I think I'll become a complete mental case."

Was it really happening? Yes! "If you really want to," cautiously. "Of course you may. Grab a taxi. You can even stay the night if you like. We'll have a regular hen party. I've got some goodies in the refrigerator, and we can send out to the liquor store for a little booze. It'll be a regular ball!"

"You're sure I won't be imposing?"

"Imposing? For heaven's sake, no. Don't be silly! Of course not." Marty felt the tears running down her cheeks. "Of course not. Why, I didn't have a thing planned for the evening. I was just going out to some dull little theater thing, and believe me when I tell you I'd much rather spend the evening with you!" Understatement of the year, she thought. "How soon can you get here?"

"I'm dressed. And I can't spend another night by myself in this lonely old house. I'll be there in fifteen minutes."

"Hurry." Marty hung up, and still crying, now uncontrollably, stripped off her nightie and started dressing.

"Oh," she whispered aloud, "beloved. Beloved visitor. Never to be lonely again. Never to be afraid of the dark, of big houses and strange noises."

Chapter X

"WE'LL GO TO MALIBU," Marty said, firmly.

It was the morning after. There had been a great deal of talk about Kirk, a subject Marty had wisely by-passed, making no comments. Let the little fool find out for herself.

"Whatever you say," Ronnie replied.

Marty shook her curls impatiently. "That's just it. You go through life saying 'whatever you say,' and what do you get? Just that, just what someone else says. You're such a child! A dear child," she added, restraining herself, nerves screaming for release, wanting to put her arms about Ronnie and confess everything. "You've got to get up on your hind legs and howl . . . like this: *oooooooh!*"

Ronnie tried it, somewhat less than successfully, and both girls broke up into laughter.

"We'll go to Malibu," Ronnie said, underscoring Marty's rebuke for failing to make up her own mind. "I've decided—we're going to Malibu. In fact, we'll stay at my place. Kirk and I . . ." she paused, realizing that she might have said the wrong thing. "Well, I have a place at Malibu. That's where we'll stay."

"You wouldn't be happy there," Marty objected firmly. "Too many memories. Wait a minute; I have a telephone number here somewhere." She rummaged through a lit-

89

ter of paper. "Here it is—now, if there's a vacancy." She dialed a number. After a preliminary conversation, she said, "That's right. No, probably just today and tonight. Thank you. We'll be there in an hour."

"Be where?" Ronnie asked.

Marty smiled. "Leave it to me. It's a nice place—private bar, pool—personally, I can't stand swimming in the ocean. Also comfort and quiet. Peace. Time to rest your fatigued emotions."

"You're being pretty dramatic," Ronnie laughed.

"Why not? I'm as excited as a kid. Look, chicky, this is my first vacation since we inaugurated the 'Movie Starlet' campaign. Maybe I'm hysterical!"

"Oh!" Ronnie put a finger to her lips, "I just remembered. I don't have anything to wear."

"Size twelve?"

"That's right."

"I've enough for both of us. Swim suits, beach wear, cocktail gowns in case we get really giddy and want to impress the natives. Let's pack, child, and be on our way!"

They lay on the sand, both well-lotioned. Marty had rubbed the lotion onto and into Ronnie, thrilling at the feel of her satin-like skin. And when Ronnie had returned the favor in kind, it was all Marty's jangled nerves could handle, just to not embrace her openly. Privately, Marty wondered if this had been a wise idea. She realized, perhaps for the first time, that she was in love—no other word for it—with this girl who trusted her so. She also realized that this was *not* the time to make any sort of pass at Ronnie, that Ronnie was a confused woman. Sympathy would go further in the long run. She sighed, resigning herself to practically *oozing* sympathy.

"Marty?"

Marty slid her sunglasses up to her forehead and turned to look at Ronnie. "Yes?"

"How do you become a career woman? Like you, I mean."

Marty pressed a finger to her own forearm to determine how much more sun she could take at this sitting. "Well," she started thoughtfully, "you take one domineering mother, one passive father and one child—me. Mix well and shake."

"Didn't you love your parents?"

"Of course, silly. I said my parents were thus and so, and that's the why of it. We never had a lot of money, but always enough. Mother ruled the roost. Dad—well, he just sort of worked and brought the money home. He didn't talk very much."

"Was he happy?"

Marty lifted a shoulder in an involuntary shrug. "What's happiness? Sure. I guess so. In his own way, I mean. Yes, I guess you could say he was happy." Oh, dear God, she said to herself, privately. She still doesn't realize that I . . . well, that I'm what I am. How can I break the news to her? How?

"Are *you* happy, Marty?"

A question. Was she happy? "Yes. I think so. Sort of miserably happy, I suppose you could say. Considering my family background."

Ronnie frowned. "Miserably happy? I'm afraid I don't understand. If you're happy, how can you be miserable?"

So. So now we're going to play the game. "Ever see a kid in front of a candy counter with a nickel in his hand? He's happy. He's got five cents. But look at all the choices. So, he's miserably happy. He's got enough money to pick out this and that, yet he can't have everything. Follow me? I guess that's the way I am, too. I've got a good position, I make good money. I should be able to stand off and point and say 'I want this or that,' but I don't do it. Put it another way. The average woman has a tremendous problem with her sex life. I mean, if you want to explore this subject for an afternoon, let's. How to attract the opposite sex, how to satisfy them after you've once attracted them. Nature's game. You either enjoy this game to the hilt, which is nature's way of doing things, or you go through the motions *without really believing any of it.*"

Ronnie took off her sunglasses, rolled over on one elbow and looked seriously at Marty, as if seeing her for the first time. "What are you trying to tell me? That you're . . . queer? A deviate? A homosexual? A lesbian?"

Marty managed to shrug from the supine position. "Darling, those are so many labels on so many different kinds of canned beans. Have I bothered you, made a pass at you? Of course not. You slept with me last night. Did I say or do anything to embarrass you? I don't think so. Stop categorizing. Above all, stop worrying about me. Isn't it enough to enjoy the sun, the fresh air? And to take a break from the daily routine? It is for me. I feel deliciously guilty being here, and I guess there's an extra spice in knowing I don't give a damn. I'm not even going to call the office. Think they'll miss us?"

"My gosh, I hope so," Ronnie said, shifting position so that the sun might tan her delectable body more evenly. She was uneasily aware of Marty's eyes devouring her, yet strangely flattered.

Marty lowered her sunglasses and lay back with mixed emotions. She genuinely admired Ronnie, Ronnie's ability, her swift-moving mind. I love her, too. The thought chased itself through her brain. Yes, I do. Careful, Marty, play it cool.

"Marty?"

"Um."

"You're a very attractive woman. Why haven't you ever tried . . . well, you know. Regular marriage?"

Marty got to her feet. "I've had about enough sun, I think. I blister easily. Coming? Let's go down the road for cocktails. I'll tell you all about it—sometime."

She extended her hand, pulled Ronnie to her feet, and they ran, laughing, into the apartment. They dressed, tossed their play clothing carelessly into the car and drove to The Key. Ronnie was a bit somber in the familiar lounge, remembering the happy times she had enjoyed with Kirk in these very surroundings.

They finished their first Martinis at the bar, and ordered two more to be served on the sun deck in privacy.

"So," Marty broke the silence. "What are your plans? About your personal life, I mean?"

Ronnie tossed her hair. "I don't know. Divorce, I guess. I really love Kirk, but I guess I'm just not cut out to be a wife. Never again. Two unhappy marriages, both of them sexually frustrating . . . well, that's enough for *this* girl. From here on, it's the bachelorette life for me. Take my fun where I find it. It just seems that marriage and Veronica don't mix. When we finish this campaign for 'Movie Starlet,' I think I'll take a long, leisurely trip. Care to come along?"

Marty laughed. "Love to, but I don't dare turn my back that long. Someone would be sure to plant a knife in it. No, my girl, my vacations are confined to an occasional week, a weekend in Manhattan, a jet flight back. I'd love to go on a cruise, but I'm afraid it's not going to happen. At least, not for a long time."

There was a shared moment of silence. Both were lost in their own thoughts. Again, Ronnie broke through.

"Marty—you are—gay, aren't you?"

"I suppose you could call it that, if you like." Cautiously, Marty, she said to herself, cautiously. Don't bitch this up.

"You don't . . . like . . . men." Straightforward.

"I don't suppose I do." A stolid answer.

"Sexually, I mean."

"Sexually," Marty agreed.

"Mind telling me why? I mean, maybe I'm in the same category and don't really know it."

Marty finished her drink and set the glass upside down on the table. "You're getting rather basic and rather . . . personal, you know."

"I'm sorry. I didn't mean to pry."

"Pry. A good word. Listen, Ronnie, I haven't pushed myself on you, correct? If you want answers, I've got them. Take a deep breath if you really want to hear my answers. Are you sure? A great many people would like to hear me expound on the subject. In the first place, I think I'm abnormal, a real nut. A pervert. I'd really rather not discuss it. Isn't it enough that I'm a damned good businesswoman? A good boss? Must I bare my personal life for the world to sort of rear back and laugh at? Even for you to laugh at? To ridicule?"

Ronnie shook her head. "No. Of course not."

"But you'd like to know. All right. Here it is, for what it's worth. I'm an adult now, remember? But the scars you suffer when you're just a kid—they stay with you all your life. Mother told me all about sex." Marty laughed, shortly. "All about *her* idea of sex, anyway. How men were dirty, how they hurt you, how it was only your *duty* to accommodate them. I bought it. Why not? I had no other standards to go by. After all, I'd heard my father and mother in the bedroom, grunting and growling. It sounds pretty disgusting to an impressionable kid, believe me. So when I went on my first heavy necking party, I was . . . well, apprehensive. It was fun, until we got down to business. Then I felt hurt. Hell, it *did* hurt. Suddenly, my mother's words came back. 'Men are dirty. Men hurt you.' Catch on? It hit me hard."

"Marty, you don't have to . . ."

"Please. I'd just as soon tell you. I've never told anyone before. So, anyway, there was this gym teacher. She was attracted to me, and I didn't know she was anything other than a regular teacher. How the hell could I? I was only fourteen years old, and I didn't know anything about lesbians. I didn't know then, but I found out in a hurry. All

94

right, why knock it? She was gentle, she was persuasive, she was accomplished. I enjoyed it. As long as I'm going to bare my soul, I enjoyed it immensely. Better than men. So, I found myself a senior in high school and out of step with the world. Men were a drag, although we didn't use that term in my day. Same thing. I caught myself having eyes for some of the other girls in my class. To tell the truth, some of them had eyes for me, even though they more than suspected my action. Well, there was a little scandal. Not much, just a little, nothing anyone could prove. So, my family sent me to a private school. For *girls,* for Christ's sake! Like turning a hog loose in a corn-crib. If I hadn't been a les up until that time, the girls' school really did the trick!" She paused, out of breath, lost in unhappy memories.

"I—I'm sorry," Ronnie offered, apologetically. "I didn't know that . . ."

"Forget it, kid. You asked me a question, and maybe for the first time in my life I'm answering the question honestly for myself. Let me talk. The sound of my own voice at a time like this sort of intrigues me. Where was I? Oh, I finally graduated from private school. I had a hell of an education. I'd been had by half the field hockey team. I got an education, all right. All the wrong things, all the wrong ways. Then, my family 'arranged' a marriage for me. Tom. From Boston, where his family spoke only to the top family, and the top family spoke only to God!

"That lasted about a month. Just for laughs, he was a screaming faggot. We weren't what you'd call an ideally mated couple, you know? I toughed it out alone for a few years. And then—" she smiled, thinking back—"and then I met this rat-fink bastard, Prince Digliano. A winner. So for two years I was a 'princess,' while he milked my family of every dime he could. Actually, he wasn't bad in the hay. I mean, all things considered. Also, he was very continental, and he picked up on my lesbian habits, never mentioned them except indirectly. But when my family closed the vault, he left me in a hurry, and that's putting it mildly. So much for the Prince, and so much for my attempts at marriage. Period, paragraph."

Ronnie let the silence fall again. Then: "And that's your experience? With men, I mean?"

Marty smiled grimly. "That's it, baby. And enough for anyone, I'd guess."

"Well, I know it's impertinent of me, but what about . . . ?"

"Girls? Hell, yes. I like girls. But I always love 'em and leave 'em. No permanent attachments for this kid."

"Gee," Ronnie said. "I know it sounds horrible, but isn't that a lonesome life?"

"The worst."

Ronnie twirled the olive on the end of her toothpick. "Don't you ever feel the . . . need for a more permanent arrangement? If that's the word."

Careful, baby, Marty told herself. "I suppose so. Unfortunately, I have a certain amount of discrimination. I have to respect someone's ability, brains, education, background and breeding. Sounds like the stud book for registered bitches, doesn't it? Still, that's the way I am."

"I can understand that."

"Can you?" Marty almost said what was in her heart but pulled herself up sharply. "Can you, indeed? I suppose you think (be still, my heart!) I'm making a pass at you? Have I ever? No."

For the first time, Ronnie considered the ramifications of the situation. "I suppose that people who know you are talking about . . . us."

"Don't be silly. I don't advertise, you know. Anyway, I'm after you for your brains and your social prestige. (Lie, black lie!) Anyway, I don't think you care to talk about or consider sex at this time."

Ronnie shuddered. "No, I don't."

"So we won't."

96

The week-end passed, somehow. Marty was in constant torment, so near to her beloved, yet separated by the very barrier of her lesbianism. She ached to hold Ronnie in her arms, to comfort her and caress her, tenderly, tenderly.

On the final night of their stay at the beach, Marty asked, "Are you going back to your house?"

Ronnie shuddered. "I don't think I could stand it, being alone in the place. It's so—so *big* without Kirk."

"You're still filing for divorce?"

Ronnie nodded, tears welling up. "Yes. It's the only thing I can do."

"I agree with you. Well, here's a suggestion: why not move in with me until the arrangements are made? I've plenty of room."

"Wonderful. If you're sure I won't be an inconvenience to you."

Marty hugged her. "Don't be silly. I'd love to have you. I get pretty lonely, too, you know. Then it's settled?" Her heart gave an exultant leap. *Soon, soon.*

"All settled," Ronnie smiled. And assured herself that she was making the correct move.

Chapter XI

"Well, by God," Marty announced happily, "that did it!"

She held up the magazine cover.

"Is that really me?" bubbled Ronnie. "I can hardly believe it!"

"It's you, all right! And they just don't make better covers than this one—nor a cover-girl as pretty or as talented as 'Movie Starlet's' Ronnie. I say this calls for a celebration. Kid, I don't know what I'd have done with this campaign if it hadn't been for you."

Ronnie took the magazine, studied it. "You'd have gotten another girl."

"She'd never have been chosen as the most popular commercial announcer of the year," Marty reminded. "A pretty face isn't everything!"

"Stop, or I'll ask for a raise."

"You need the money like a hole in your head, but I've got news for you, Ron—you have a raise coming through. I saw to that. Gosh, I'm proud of you; I guess that makes me say, in a way, that I'm proud of myself for "discovering' you. Hey, everybody: take the rest of the day off. We've got it made!"

The entire advertising and promotional staff of "Movie

Starlet" crowded around to offer their congratulations, and Ronnie said, stoutly:

"Nonsense. It was a team job. Why, it couldn't have happened if you weren't working behind me. If any one person deserves the credit, it's Marty. Don't forget, she went ahead when everyone said it was a bad promotion, a bad trade name, an attempt to hit a poor segment of the market and everything else. I say, let's thank Marty!"

Marty grunted. "I say, let's all go get drunk!"

Except for the office boy, this was a swinging suggestion. Marty named a spot on The Strip and everyone hustled to get coats, wraps, hats. There was one other reluctant celebrator—Dianne Van Lau, who'd just come into the office, frantically jealous (without good reason, yet) of Ronnie.

"Hi," she said. "Where's everyone going?"

Marty scarcely noticed her. "We're celebrating a small triumph. The 'Movie Starlet' campaign has just reached a climax."

Dianne grinned, knowingly. "And you, darling? Are you reaching climaxes yet? With your little friend, Ronnie?"

"You're a bitch. A complete bitch."

"I know. And I like it that way. I thought maybe we could get together tonight. Later. Like old times, you know?"

"That," Marty said firmly, "will be the day! Forget it. Go get another husband or something. Get out of my life. Let me alone."

Ronnie was returning to the office, unaware of the by-play. "That one, eh?" Dianne mouthed, sourly. "Lots of luck. Do you really think you can replace her husband? Darling Kirk? I doubt it. I doubt it very much."

"You'd look even more lovely with a couple of deep scratches on your face." That was a flat statement, and Marty meant it.

"Well," Dianne said, smiling falsely but firmly. "Here she is. Miss 'Movie Starlet' herself. Hello, Ronnie."

Ronnie was a bit uncertain. "Oh—hello, there. Joining the party? We're sort of celebrating."

"I heard. No, I don't think so. I'll leave you—*girls* to yourselves. I don't think, somehow, that you need any more company." Dianne turned on her heels and left.

"What is that all about?" Ronnie asked Marty.

Marty shrugged. "My past is catching up. I hope you don't mind."

"This afternoon, I don't mind anything. I'm floating on cloud nine. Care to join me?"

Marty threw her wrap around her shoulders, grasped Ronnie by the arm. "Hell, no! Let's go get the troops drunk. Later, we'll have dinner and maybe we can analyze this thing—this success with 'Movie Starlet.'"

They left, arm in arm.

Then the rains came.

In Los Angeles, native sons and daughters will stoutly proclaim that they've never heard a thunderstorm.

This is nonsense, of course. One can *rarely* hear a thunderstorm, or one can sleep through a thunderstorm without being aware of it, and, in all honesty, thunderstorms are rare, but they happen. Every year. And when they do, they're humdingers. This one was no exception. Ronnie and Marty had retired to separate bedrooms, and the rains came. With the rain came thunder and lightning, and when the first streak of lightning split the sky, Ronnie was up and screaming.

Marty, attired in only a sheer gown, appeared grumpily at the door to Ronnie's bedroom. "Nightmare?" she inquired, politely.

Outside, there was a regular cloudburst.

"No," Ronnie said. "No, it's just that I'm afraid of thunder and lightning. I can't help it. Ever since I was a little girl, I've been afraid of thunder and lightning."

"Donner und blitzen," Marty remarked. "Well, child, come on into mother's bed. For what good it will do, I'll protect you. Maybe we'll be struck together, or something."

Ronnie meekly complied, and when they were snuggled together under the covers, Marty had to call on all her resources so as to restrain her impulses. Oh, delightful, beautiful girl! Oh, my love, my life!

It was almost a welcome relief when the door chime rang, followed by a pounding. Marty got up, gratefully, went to the door. Without removing the chain, she opened it cautiously. She glanced at her watch. It was three in the morning. Marty was reasonably drunk, as was Ronnie. It was Kirk at the door, and Kirk was more than reasonably drunk. Kirk, to put it briefly, was stoned. Incoherent.

Thoughtfully, Marty opened the door.

Kirk, drenched, sodden and very, very angry, flung himself in dramatically.

"My wife," he shouted. "Where's my wife, you lousy dyke?"

"Stay right there and drip in one spot," Marty advised him. "I'll get her for you." She went to the bedroom door. "Ronnie—someone to see you."

Ronnie came out, knuckling her eyes like a small child. "Who, Marty? Oh!" as she saw Kirk.

Kirk took one look at his wife. "Get your clothes on," he ordered, sternly. "You're getting out of here, away from this stinking lesbian."

"I'm not going anywhere with you, Kirk. Not in your condition."

"Oh? You're leaving, or I'm calling the cops."

Marty thrust herself forward. "You do that, mister. Did you hear what Ronnie said? She doesn't want to go with you. You just call the cops. What are you going to tell them? That I'm a lesbian, that I've seduced your wife? Forget it. Your wife is staying with a girl friend because she doesn't trust you. Because you left her. Maybe, to tell the truth, buster, I love her more than you do. I love her so much that *I'm* going to call the police and tell them you forced your way into my apartment. How does that grab you, mister? You better start walking!"

Kirk made a strangling sound in his throat. "Ronnie?" It was a plea.

"Marty's right. Maybe she *does* love me more than you. You'd better leave, Kirk."

He wrenched open the door, turned to say something, then shook his head. He slammed the door behind him, and they could hear him stumbling down the stairs. Marty locked the door carefully and turned to Ronnie with a strange expression on her face.

"And that's . . . that."

Ronnie nodded. "Yes. That's that."

Marty turned off the lamp. "Coming back to bed?"

"Yes. Marty, be kind to me, and very gentle. I've never . . ."

Marty went to the younger girl, held her closely, kissed her. "I know. Please, darling, if you'd rather, we'll just forget the whole thing. I don't want you to do anything you don't want to do. Ever."

Ronnie returned the kiss. Somehow, it felt good and right and fine, somehow.

In bed, it was the same. Marty forgot all her wiles, all the tricks she'd employed in the past for her many and varied conquests. This was, she told herself, true love.

Ronnie submitted, wonderingly, then with increasing passion. It was more than satisfactory for both girls. Neither felt a sense of guilt.

There was one small doubt in Marty's mind. After an exhausted Ronnie fell to sleep in her arms, Marty wondered if she'd ever truly possess this wonderful creature.

The hell with it, she decided. Let tomorrow take care of itself. Tonight, I'm the happiest woman in the world, holding my true love, my one love here in my arms.

It continued to rain.

Chapter XII

IT WAS still raining Tuesday morning, even as late as Kirk Ward got to his office. A prim Miss Bradley looked disapprovingly, he thought, at his somewhat hung-over appearance, and he said, inwardly, the hell with it. Ward tried to read his mail, but the unpleasant picture of the preceding night kept intervening. Finally, unable to concentrate on network problems, he decided to do something on his own. He pressed the intercom switch.

"Miss Bradley?"

"Yes, sir!" Neat, prompt, efficient, disapproving.

"Get me Joe Katzmann, please. At Persons, Smith and Nash."

"Yes, Mr. Ward. At once."

In moments, Kirk was talking to Katzmann. "Joe, what do you know about a firm called 'Amour Cosmetics'? They've recently marketed a new line called 'Movie Starlet.'"

"It's a hot property, Kirk. Very good."

"Is it on the Big Board?"

"No. It's strictly over-the-counter. You want some?"

"I want control, Joe."

Katzmann whistled. "Control? Jesus, Kirk, I don't know. The way the common stock is going—"

"That's all I'm interested in. Forget preferred. Joe, I

really want actual, physical, control. How long will it take, how much will it take, and how soon can you turn it over to me?"

"Please, Kirk, not so fast. You know how big an order you're giving me? Let me get my folder—hold on." He was gone from the telephone four or five minutes. "All right, Kirk, here it is, as of closing yesterday: fifty-three per cent of all outstanding common stock has been issued and sold. Forty-seven per cent is available. A—let me see—a Martha Browning owns about eighteen or nineteen per cent of all issued stock, which actually gives her voting control. What do you want me to do?"

"Can you pick up the forty-seven per cent?"

"At a price, yes."

"Good. Do that. Now, I want you to sniff around and find me some more stock. I want an honest-to-God, hard-core fifty-one per cent of all common stock. I don't want to get involved in proxy battles or anything like that. I want absolute control."

"Kirk, it's going to cost a lot of money."

"I know. You just said that. Do it."

"We may have to sell some of your other stuff."

"Go ahead. Do whatever's necessary."

"Thank you for the order, Kirk. My commission on this one's going to make some people very happy— my two ex-wives."

Kirk hung up, thoughtfully, and tried to get back to his office routine. It was, he discovered, impossible to concentrate. He called Miss Bradley and told her to cancel all his appointments for the day, that he was going to be out. No, he didn't know where he could be reached, but he'd call in. Miss Bradley's disapproval was evidenced in the way she said, "Yes, Mr. Ward."

He leaned back in his chair, wearily massaging his forehead. God, he was something more than hung-over. He was emotionally drained, exhausted.

He went out his private exit into the bright Hollywood sunlight, walking aimlessly along Vine Street.

Doctor James Pelley, M.D., Ph.D., shook his head. "Kirk, I can't help you. I'm a clinical psychologist, not a miracle worker, certainly not a marriage counselor. If your suspicions about Ronnie are true, I suspect she's in more need of help than you, anyway. Let me ask you: do you still love her, despite this homosexual fling she appears to be taking?"

"No. Yes. Oh, hell, Jim, I don't know."

The doctor tapped his pencil on the desk top, softly. "I can tell you this much: if half of what you've told me is the truth, and if Ronnie is in the clutch of a confirmed lesbian, you drove her there. And I'm very much afraid that only you can get her back."

"But can I? I've heard that once a woman experiences the embraces of a lesbian she's ruined for men forever."

"Not unless she was already homosexually oriented."

"Now, what the hell is *that* supposed to mean?"

Pelley stood up. "For one thing, it means that you're taking up too much of my time. For another, it means that I'm not going to be able to give you a short course in psychology or psychiatry." He leveled a finger at the younger man. "If you love Ronnie, if you really want to help her, you'd better get busy and do something about it."

"You know," Kirk said slowly, "I think maybe I am doing something about it."

They shook hands. Kirk ate an early lunch and went back to his office.

Katzmann called on Wednesday afternoon. "I've got that forty-seven per cent. Now, Kirk, that gives you virtual control. I bought it through several dummies, so they wouldn't suspect a raid, but I'm afraid the word is out."

"I don't want 'virtual' control, Joe. I want absolute, actual physical control. Fifty-one per cent."

"Kirk, I'm trying to explain. That next four per cent is going to cost you damned near as much as the original purchase. I don't think you'll need it, that's all."

"For what I have in mind, I'll need it, all right," Kirk said, grimly. "Get it for me."

"I'll have to sell off some of your blue chip stuff, Kirk."

"Sell it. Don't dicker. Get me that other four per cent, Joe, and get it fast."

"You're the boss."

Katzman called back shortly before noon next day. "Let's meet for lunch."

"Did you get it?"

"I got it. You paid through the nose."

"Tell me about it at noon. The Derby?"

"Right. Noon sharp."

Kirk hung up, took a deep breath. For better or worse, it was a *fait accompli*.

They waited for their Martinis. After they'd arrived, Katzmann handed over a leatherette zip case to Kirk. "Very interesting little folder in there," he observed. "Close to a million and a half bucks. Tell me the truth—*are* you going to raid this company?"

"Is it showing a profit?"

"A damned nice one. That vice-president they've got, that Martha Browning, is largely responsible, too. You mean to tell me you bought this outfit without knowing anything about it?" He started at Kirk, incredulously.

"There are a few things more important than a nice profit, or even money."

Katzmann laughed, shortly. "Not in my line of work. Well, you've got your company, I've got a hell of a nice commission, some of which I may be able to hang onto. Let's have another Martini, then order."

When lunch finally arrived, Kirk toyed idly with his food, lost in thought. His next step was going to be a big one, and possibly disastrous. And this time, he wouldn't be gambling with money, but with human values.

"Joe," he said, "Do me a favor. You have a list of all the other stockholders in the firm?"

"What? Oh, sure. Something in mind?"

"Yes." He put down his coffee cup, lit a cigarette. "I want you to call a meeting of the stockholders for tomorrow morning. We'll use your firm's board room, if it's okay with you."

"Sure. On one condition—I get to watch. I've never seen anyone actually take physical control of a company before. There'll be fireworks, won't there?"

"Yes," Kirk said, softly, without special emphasis. "Yes, I rather expect there'll be fireworks. Oh, and you'll furnish me with a secretary for the occasion?"

"Be my pleasure. What time?"

"Make it early. Eight-thirty."

"Aha! Weakened resistance at that hour, hey?"

"You could put it that way."

"Boy," Katzmann grinned, "I'll bet there are going to be some unhappy people an hour after that meeting starts."

"It won't take that long. All right, Joe. Hop to it."

"Here, I'll get the check. I might as well get some pleasure out of my commission on this deal before my ex-wives move in for the kill."

Kirk sat up late that night, deciding just what he was going to do next morning, Friday, and what the probable effect might be on his home life.

Aside from Kirk and Katzmann—and the secretary—there were six people, including a shocked Martha Browning in the board room for the early morning meeting. Kirk merely acknowledged the introductions with a courteous nod, making no attempt to remember names. These people were relatively unimportant. Secretary of the corporation was a mousy-looking individual who owned about five per cent of the shares. He fussily opened a book and read the minutes of the last meeting. Kirk closed his ears to the words, let the voice drone on and come to a halt. Kirk sat up, rapped a knuckle on the table for attention.

"I'm out of order," he said apologetically, "but only for a moment, I think. I have, in the past few days, acquired a hard fifty-one per cent of this firm. I'm sure you are aware of the implications. I have my own auditor," he glanced at his watch, "at the offices going over the books. Mr. Secretary, perhaps you would be kind enough to give me a projected picture of our profit for the current year? Just a rough one."

The little man beamed, delighted to give the big investor the benefit of his knowledge. "Yes, indeed." He cleared his throat. "I'm delighted to say that, based on sales to date and probable futures, we'll clear something like three hundred thousand dollars for the current year. Give or take a few thousand dollars, of course. This despite the expense of new packaging and a terribly expensive but successful advertising campaign. For our 'Movie Starlet' line. Miss Browning has done a magnificent job, and I must add in all fairness that it was done against our judgment. She proved herself right."

"I see. Well, that works out very well. Three hundred thousand is the figure I had in mind for my salary as President, Chairman and General Manager."

Katzmann laughed aloud, as the people gathered around the table voiced their objections. Only Marty said nothing, waiting for the rest of it.

A portly man at the table spoke up. "Mr. Ward, you simply cannot do this thing."

Kirk tapped his portfolio which lay before him. "There's fifty-one per cent of the stock which says I can. I haven't quite finished yet. I will buy your stock, any or all of it, if any of you feel dissatisfied. At," he added, unsmiling, "par value, of course. You can make up your minds as to your course of action at your leisure, naturally, and Mr. Katzmann here, is fully authorized to negotiate any such transactions in my name. Oh—one more thing. Miss Browning," he glanced carelessly at Marty, whose nostrils were pinched, white, "Congratulations on an admirable campaign. Highly commendable. You'll go far. I hardly think our firm is large enough for your *many* talents, however. I've arranged with my auditor to prepare you a severance check. There will also be a substantial cash bonus for you—if you decide to turn your stock back to the company. At par value."

"You son of a bitch," Marty hissed. *"You dirty son of a bitch!"*

"Hardly the language of a lady, Miss Browning. However, I suppose you're the best judge of your ladylike attributes. Well, gentlemen, I think that's all for today. If there are no objections, I move this meeting be adjourned. I'll send a memo to each of you next week, stating my personal aims and policies for the future conduct of business."

He sat impassively as the room emptied. Katzmann shook his head when they were alone. "Boy, you're a goddamned pirate! I *knew* you were going to raid the company! You shouldn't have let that Browning dame go, though. Hell, she's the one who pumped up this company!"

"Joe," Kirk said, coldly, "stick to your stocks and bonds. The Browning woman is worth a hell of a lot more to me out of the company than in it. Let me know the minute she dumps her stocks, too. That's important."

Oh, dear God, Kirk thought to himself as he left for a waiting taxi, let this work out the way I want it to. It *must!*

Chapter XIII

MARTY'S RAGE was a cold and ugly thing. It possessed her completely, eradicating even the love she'd felt for Ronnie. No divorce, no soft white arms, no sweet, perfumed lips, could remove the stench of Kirk Ward from this woman. Kirk had stripped Marty of the proud garment of success she had worn so long. He had exposed her frailities as a woman, and as a woman she had no weapon with which to fight him.

As a bull dyke, she had his wife. So, through no fault of her own, Ronnie became identified with the foe, and Marty selected her tender young trust as the battleground.

The fact that Ronnie had turned to Marty's arms every night since that rainy evening when Kirk had tried to force her into leaving with him, was quickly forgotten, or buried deeply beneath the icy barrier surrounding Marty's heart. Forgotten also was the warm tenderness of this first true love affair. Nothing remained except the desire for revenge.

When she arrived home from the meeting, Ronnie was not there. Marty was grateful for the opportunity to compose herself—the time in which to disguise her hatred for Ronnie and make her plans for destroying her. She mixed a pitcher full of Martinis, and as she sipped one from a chilled, crystal cocktail glass Marty mulled over the problem. Idea after idea ran through her head, only to be discarded. One of them refused to stay discarded however, and the fourth or fifth time it forced its way back into her mind Marty gave it her full attention.

Why not? If her original estimate of Ronnie as a very sensitive, albeit confused little girl, had been correct, this plan could destroy her as effectively as her husband had destroyed Marty.

The Song! Despite the many years she had lived with her lesbianism; despite the many affairs, some thrilling, others sordid, The Song always tore her to pieces. She never visited the place that she didn't come away feeling dirty, evil, almost completely perverted. If, Marty hummed to herself, the place affects *me* that way, it ought to just about devastate Mrs. Kirk Ward.

When Ronnie arrived home, Marty had showered, and was sipping another Martini. She hadn't dressed for the evening as yet, but sat curled up on the couch wearing an ice-blue satin robe. Ronnie was delighted to find her there, and ran across the room to kiss her gently. Marty forced herself to return the kiss, but didn't try to pretend a passion she no longer felt. Instead, she disengaged herself from Ronnie's arms, stood up and walked to the small bar. There, she poured two Martinis—a first for Ronnie, a third for herself.

"Do you remember," she asked as she handed Ronnie the drink, "the day you were asking me about being a lesbian?"

Ronnie looked up sharply, an expression of hurt bewilderment fleeting across her face. "Of course I do, Marty—but why should you bring that up now? You must know how much the past few nights have changed my ideas on the subject. Still, no matter what we've meant to each other, I hate to think of that word in connection with myself."

Marty turned her back and grinned. She'd thought Ronnie would have exactly this reaction. She was happy

111

with it because it meant that her plan of action for the evening would fulfill its purpose.

"Finish your drink and take your shower. Then, Ronnie, I want you to put on your most beautiful cocktail dress. We're going out for the evening."

Ronnie misunderstood her completely. She thought Marty had made the sudden offer by way of apology for introducing a subject unpleasant to Ronnie. It wasn't until she came out of the small dressing room, ready for cocktails and dinner at a Strip restaurant that she learned just how wrong she'd been.

Marty stood arrogantly in the middle of the living room. She was wearing the jeans, boots and leather jacket of her bull dyke moods.

Ronnie gasped in dismayed astonishment. "Marty! What in the world—"

"It's about time, little one, that you face the seamier aspects of your new-found sex life. We have to conceal our affair from everyone in our own group, but there's a place—not too far from here—where we can be what we are without shame. Where I can boast about my conquest—just like a man does when he's made a new chick. We're going there tonight, baby."

Ronnie's eyes widened as she listened to the ugly words —words spoken deliberately, with malice aforethought —words which were forcing her to accept the mantle of Lesbos; a mantle for which she was almost completely unprepared. Tears welled into her eyes, overflowing and streaming softly down her face. At the sight of them, Marty strode rapidly across the room and slapped her viciously across the mouth.

"Pour yourself another drink, baby, and cut the crying. It's a little late for tears. You came to me willingly. You've been with me every night this week. Now I want to introduce you to some friends of mine, and I don't want you looking like a drowned cat!"

Ronnie's tears stopped, but she moved toward the bar

like someone in a deep trance. Actually, she couldn't believe the words Marty was saying, nor even the sting of her hand upon her face. This is, she told herself, a very bad dream. It's my conscience getting to me. I'm ashamed of what I've done with Marty, and this dream is my mind warning me to stop. As she poured the Martini for herself, she said a silent prayer that she would waken before the dream became uglier.

Marty watched her curiously. She hadn't really expected Ronnie to stop weeping so quickly. She had expected more of a fight from her. I hope, she told herself, that this woman isn't going to enjoy this night. If she does, I lose my revenge on her husband, and I'll probably also lose the girl herself.

To Ronnie, she said merely, "Drink it down, Ronnie. I want to get out of here. Things should be getting into high gear at The Song, and I don't want *you* to miss any of the action!"

Ronnie did as she was told.

When they reached the small, strange car, Ronnie was still too deeply in shock to notice it. When they arrived at The Song, Ronnie looked at the ugly street, and the garish club, but remained silent. Marty was getting somewhat worried. Christ, she thought, I hope this thing isn't going to backfire on me.

She helped Ronnie out of the little car, and taking her arm in true butch fashion, walked proudly through the entrance of the club, aware of every eye in the place turning toward her. She'd never brought her own date to The Song before. Ronnie Ward was, of course, even more than just another date. She was rich, famous and very beautiful. You could feel the collective desire stirring as the gathered lesbians drank in her beauty. Marty felt a quiver in Ronnie's arm as she led her toward the bar. Good. She wasn't as calm as she appeared. The place was already getting to her, and the evening hadn't as yet begun.

"Hey, Bobbie!" Marty called out to the obviously impressed faggot behind the bar. "Give me and my little femme a couple of great big drinks." She patted Ronnie's firmly curved buttocks in a gesture of ownership, and sat proudly beside her. Looking around the room, seeing the naked lust in the eyes fixed upon Ronnie, she gave a triumphant laugh, "Suffer, you bitches! Sweat it out the hard way. This one is all mine. You can look, but keep your goddamned hands to yourself!"

Bobbie served their drinks, looking in amazement at the usually well-mannered Marty. Good lord, he thought, she's acting as mean as Gretch. I never would have thought Ronnie Ward would go along with this kind of treatment. But then, you never can tell. I have, he added to himself, a bad feeling about this night. A real bad feeling.

Half an hour later, Ronnie still hadn't said a word, and Marty was becoming disconcerted with the lack of attention the others were giving them. She never should have been so rough when they first came in, she thought. I've scared the damn fools off, she whispered to herself, and that's the last thing I wanted.

"Bobbie-boy," she called to the scared bartender. "What say you give the house a drink? On me, and my femme. She's kind of new to the place, and she'd like to make some new friends. Tell the kids not to be scared— they should come on over for an introduction."

Bobbie thought privately that Marty must have gone off her rocker, but he knew better than to try to cross her in any way. He delivered drinks and Marty's message to a group at another end of the bar, then to several tables toward the back. It wasn't too long before several of the rougher-looking dykes were at the bar beside Ronnie and Marty. Marty had just completed the introduction when Gretch, her arch-foe, the stripper and Betty the femme whore walked in the front door. This, Marty thought, is exactly what I've been waiting for.

"Gretch, you wretch," Marty called out her greeting. "Come on up here and meet the sweetest little chickie in the world. I've been telling her *all* about you, and she thinks she might dig you good!"

Gretch, as usual, was near complete drunkenness. Marty's words failed to sink through the alcoholic stupor, but Ronnie's beauty made the grade. "Where," the bull dyke bellowed, "did you pick up that piece of treasure?" Without waiting for an answer she pushed her way through the women around Ronnie, and grabbing her by her soft hair, implanted a sloppy, garlic and wine-laden kiss fully upon her mouth.

Ronnie looked as though she was going to faint, or throw up—possibly both.

Marty ordered another round for all the women paying court to Ronnie, reaching across the bar for Ronnie's purse. She took the wallet from it, pushed the purse back. Then she pulled a bill from the wallet, paid the bartender and put the wallet in her own hip pocket. The stripper and Betty stood away from the bar, watching their "man" go all out on the make for Ronnie. Marty smiled with satisfaction, and quietly stood up from the bar stool, and walked across the room to the "ladies room." Inside, she took Ronnie's wallet from her pocket and stuffed it deeply into the waste disposal basket, covering it with the soiled tissues and paper towels already near the top. Then she climbed out of the back window and walked around the block. As she drove away, she glanced back once at the ugly building. She laughed loudly, and her voice rang challengingly through the deserted streets. "Don't thank me for the lovely evening you're about to have, Ronnie Ward. Save your thanks for that stinkin' husband of yours!"

The sound of her laughter continued, but Marty could barely see the street signals through the veil of tears which covered her eyes.

115

Marty had been absent for over an hour when the fact impressed itself upon Ronnie. The dazed, heartsick woman faced this new insult with the air of a sleepwalker about to waken. The facade of protective disbelief began to melt away, and Ronnie looked with horror at her surroundings. The final wrench into full consciousness was the pressure of Gretch's hand upon her soft breast. This can't be happening, but it is, Ronnie screamed inwardly. Then, as on that fateful evening not too long ago, came the words: *Where is Kirk?*

With the words came the need for immediate action. Ronnie pulled herself from the ugly hands pawing about, and reached for her purse. She realized at once that her wallet was missing, and she realized almost immediately that Marty must have taken it. What, she wondered with deep sickness, have I ever done to Marty that she should treat me this way? Is this the way of a woman gone gay? Are they all like this? Will I end up like this? Oh, dear God, *where is Kirk?*

As she lifted her eyes from the emptied purse, she saw the gaze of the bartender, fixed understandingly upon her. He will help me, she thought, he might be a faggot, but he must have some kind of manhood left. "Excuse me, please," she spoke softly to the dykes around her, "I must make a telephone call." As they moved forward ominously, Ronnie realized she was in big trouble if they should spot her revulsion toward them. Calling upon every bit of acting ability she'd ever possessed, Ronnie smiled coquettishly, "It won't change our *fun* tonight, don't worry. It's a business call, something I forgot to handle today. Once I get it off my mind, I'm free for the rest of the night!"

The group moved back to let her pass. She walked along the bar toward the cash register, and the watching faggot. "Please, help me," Ronnie whispered softly. "Marty took my money, and I have to make a phone call. Please, lend me the money. And let me have a book of

116

matches, or something with the address on it. I don't even know where I am."

Bobbie glanced casually toward the dykes at the end of the bar. If they saw him give Ronnie money, and she used it to get someone down here to help her out of their clutches, God help him. For a moment, he was tempted to refuse, but another look at Ronnie changed his mind. He'd always hated the dykes, particularly Gretch and her followers. This was his big chance to get even. He took it.

Leaning over the bar, he pointed toward a door near the back of the bar. "Go to the ladies room first," he whispered. "I'll pretend to make a phone call while you're gone. When you come out, go to the phone booth. I'll leave some change and the address in the booth."

Ronnie understood his problem, although later she could never explain just how, or why. When she came out of the restroom, Bobbie was just leaving the phone booth for the bar. She closed the door to the booth, and picked up one of the dimes lying beside the phone. As she dialed the number of Kirk's office, she found herself praying the night service could put her through to him directly. She still had no idea of where he was living. The joy she felt when his own voice answered the phone was an actual physical emotion. She tried to hold back the tears, failing completely. "Kirk, oh Kirk, please. Please, darling, come save me. It's so dirty, so foul—Kirk—"

Without asking any explanation (Kirk knew when Ronnie sounded as she did at this point, she was in really big trouble), he said, "Where are you?"

She managed to hold back the tears long enough to read the address of The Song from the note Bobbie had left. "And hurry, Kirk. Please hurry. I'm actually terrified."

"Hang on, darling. I'll get there as fast as the law will allow me!" He hung up before he heard Ronnie's last words.

117

"I love you, Kirk Ward. I always will."

She stayed in the phone booth about ten minutes, hoping to remain within its comparatively secure walls until Kirk arrived. But the dykes at the bar were growing restless, and finally Ronnie forced herself to get up and walk out of the booth, across the room, back to the bar. She prayed all the way.

She was still praying when the front door opened and she saw Kirk standing belligerently in the entrance. Then Ronnie broke. She screamed his name loudly—once. As he reached her side, she fell, unconscious, into his arms.

The dykes looked on with vicious hatred as Kirk picked his wife up in his arms, glared once at the ugly women, then turned and walked out of the place.

"Just wait," bellowed Gretch to the room in general. "Just you wait till that Marty bitch shows up here again! She's gonna pay big for this little joke!"

The room's silence was loud with assent. Martha Browning was in trouble.

Chapter XIV

MARTY SAT at one end of the bar, still in a butch costume. Dianne Van Lau sat at the other. The barbed insults of the other butches had long since passed away, and now it was only the pair of them, in a bitching mood, reading each other's beads.

Bobbie, the gay bartender, turned on the television set in an effort to cut out the sound of their voices. I'm actually getting physically ill, he said to himself. I need a job, but I'm going to quit this one if I even get a *rumor* of another one!

Both Marty and Dianne were drunk, and somewhat maudlin.

Dianne sneered. "Give up, buster? When are you coming back to momma?"

"I'd rather die, you perverted bitch!"

Dianne beckoned to Bobbie. "Give that big bull dyke a drink on me."

Marty looked up, blearily. "Shove it. You know where. I'll buy my own drinks."

Bobbie stomped a foot. "Well, I *never!*" he exclaimed in outrage.

Marty ignored everyone and watched the television set. A commercial came on the screen, and suddenly Ronnie's clean, cool beauty washed across the room.

Dianne laughed raucously. Marty laid her head on the bar top and sobbed, brokenly, great gulping sobs.

"Miss her, huh?" Dianne exulted. "Good! Old friends are the best friends after all!"

Marty raised a tear-streaked face. "Drop dead, you bitch!"

"Language!" Bobbie chided. "Language! Let's hold it down, shall we?"

On the way home, Kirk reassured Ronnie, but communed with himself. Don't get superior, he advised himself. It would be so easy, and Ronnie would probably accept it. No recriminations. Just be glad she's come back, that she wanted to come back, that she called you. Above all, be glad things worked out as they did. So you wrecked a company, blew better than a million dollars doing it. Was it worth it?

Yes!

At home, he parked in the circular drive, tenderly helped Ronnie out of the car.

"It . . . it looks so *good!*" she exclaimed. "I'm home, Kirk. Really home. Am I . . . welcome?"

"Of course you are," he said, gravely. "I'm a bit overwhelmed by the sight of the old homestead myself. Would you like me to carry you over the threshold, like a new bride?"

She shook her head. "No. I'd rather pretend that none of these ugly things ever happened. Let's just walk in, have a drink and talk it out. It's been something of a nightmare for me, Kirk."

He fished for his house keys. "For me, too, darling."

In the coolness of the entry hall, Ronnie stopped, looking around, sniffing the air. "It's . . . it's so different, Kirk. This was the biggest, ugliest, most frightening place in the world without you. Now, it's like a little rose-covered cottage. God, when I think of what I've done . . ."

Kirk placed a finger over her lips. "Hush. That's

enough of that. It's over now. Let's both look on it as a bad dream. I haven't exactly been a winner, you know."

They entered the living room. She turned to Kirk. "Darling, am I going to need . . . well, *treatment?* Psychiatric care?"

Kirk went to the refrigerator behind the bar; fought the battle of the frozen ice cube tray, finally managed to get one loose and started to make drinks for them. He handed her a drink. "No," he said carefully. "No, I shouldn't think so. Perhaps I do."

She looked at him with big eyes peering over the rim of her glass. "Can things ever be the same between us, Kirk? Can you forgive me? What I've done? I know it's horrible."

"Horrible? I suppose so, in a way. But Ronnie, it was my fault, not yours. I drove you to it. Suppose we forget it and start again."

"I can't quite forget it, just like that. Kirk, I went to Marty's arms. She didn't seduce me or . . . or anything like that. I was just so lonesome. Whatever you do, don't blame her."

"I only blame myself for the whole incident. And that's just what it was . . . an incident."

"She was horrible tonight. Marty, I mean. She's never been cruel before, but somehow, it seemed as if she couldn't hurt me enough."

Kirk flushed, finished his drink and mixed another. "I'm afraid I've been drinking a little too much since you . . . left. I'll get over it."

Ronnie sat on the sofa, kicked off her shoes, wriggling her toes luxuriously. "Of course," she agreed, absently. "Kirk, do you know that Marty is really a very unhappy person?"

"Must we discuss her any more? I think she's hurt both of us enough . . ."

"Oh, no. You mustn't say that, Kirk. What we did, we did. She was later."

"I'm sure. Still, must we *discuss* her?"

Ronnie looked up, resolutely. "Yes, I think we must."

Marty was very drunk. So was Dianne, but not nearly so drunk as Marty.

Marty crooned softly to herself, possessing that weird alcoholic facility of total recall.

Peer of the Gods he seemeth to me, the blissful

Man who sits and gazes at thee before him,

Close beside thee sits and in silence

Hears thee, silvery speaking,

Laughing Love's low laughter, oh this, oh this

Only stirs the troubled heart in my breast to tremble!"

Dianne sneered aloud. "What the hell's that supposed to mean?"

Marty turned a drunken but knowing eye. "That? You stupid bitch, that's the 'Ode to Athis' by Sappho. She wrote it after she lost her lover to a man. I doubt if you ever heard of Sappho. You're more the Beatle type. I will also mention," she enunciated carefully, "that you are a no-good, goddamned freak. For the record. Let's get it in the record by all means."

"Bitch," Dianne said.

"Ladies," Bobbie cried. "Language. Language!"

The club was starting to fill up with the late crowd. Bobbie hoped there'd be no more of this, but he didn't have a lot of hope. It looked like a lousy few hours ahead. "The moon must be full," he said aloud, to no one in particular. He hoped that Heathcliffe would be in soon, as promised. He could certainly use a little moral support.

Ronnie and Kirk had made love. It wasn't as satisfactory as it might have been, but both knew the reason. There was still the dark cloud of Marty between them, of Marty . . . and of lesbianism. Still, it was good, and they felt intimate. Close.

"I feel like purring," Ronnie announced.

"Yes," Kirk said, lighting a cigarette. "I know what you mean. Welcome home."

She squeezed his arm. "What about dinner? Hungry?"

He glanced at the watch he was still wearing. "It's late, but I'm ravenous. I don't suppose there's anything here, though?"

"We could go out. An all-night coffee shop. Or Barney's."

He yawned. "I'm so *damned* tired. It's been a long few days, baby. I don't know whether I'm tiredest or hungriest."

"I'm hungriest," she said, promptly. "Get out of bed, lazy one. Let's throw something on and grab some eggs or something. I've got to go to the store first thing tomorrow."

He kissed her neck. "Whatever you say, princess. *Then* can we come home and get some sleep?"

"We can indeed." She threw the covers off, climbed out of bed. He exulted at her sleek beauty. Marty was, momentarily, forgotten.

She slipped into panties, bra, a pair of capris. A brushed-wool sweater. She ran a comb through her hair, applied a dab of lipstick. She was ready. Kirk was still groaning on the edge of the bed. "I thought women were always slow getting dressed," she scoffed. "Come on, pappy. Put something on. And bring the wallet. I'm starved. I warn you, this little expedition is going to cost money!"

Kirk dressed rapidly, wearing slacks, loafers, a knit shirt. He slipped his watch off, rinsed his face and combed his hair. He came back into the living room. "Ready."

"Me too."

They went out the front door, hand in hand. Kirk put down the top on the convertible. They drove in companionable silence. Kirk switched on the car radio, and Ronnie hummed along with the music. She looked very tiny curled up on the seat. And very dear.

Kirk smiled to himself. It was good, and it would be better.

They had an unusual meal at Barney's Beanery. Onion soup, ham and eggs, Irish coffee.

Both lit cigarettes. Kirk paid Theresa, the waitress *cum* cook, and they went out to the car.

Ronnie placed a restraining hand on his arm as he prepared to turn on the ignition. "Do you mind if we just talk for a few minutes?"

"Any particular subject?"

"Yes. Marty."

Kirk restrained himself with an effort. "Perhaps tomorrow would be better."

Ronnie shook her head. "No. I think now is the time. You think of her as some kind of a monster, don't you?"

"Ronnie, for God's sake—haven't we had enough of Marty for one day?"

"She's a very intelligent person, Kirk. And very sensitive. And not at all to blame for what she is. She was driven to it. By her family. It could have happened to anyone, Kirk."

Kirk digested this. It had certainly happened to Ronnie, and he'd certainly been the one to drive her to it. This was undeniable. Still—"I suppose you think she's in love with you? Still?"

Ronnie looked at Kirk, steadily. "No, Kirk. That's the tragedy of it, don't you see? She can't truly love. She *thinks* she can love, she tries to take the man's role, but it just isn't possible. She's living a strange, sad parody of life and love. She's worked like a dog to establish herself in business, Kirk. She's a brilliant person, but she has this horrible blind spot, this affliction. You know all she's done for 'Movie Starlet,' when everyone said she was wrong. She'll do more. But her personal life is a mess. A mess she can't help. I had you to turn to again, but she has, literally, no one and nothing. Except her job."

Kirk took a deep breath. How much should he tell

Ronnie? Everything. That was the only way to operate. Tell the truth, the whole truth. Tell about the stock purchase, the brutal firing.

"Light another cigarette," he told Ronnie, "and sit back. Brace yourself. I've got a kind of confession to make. I'm not sure you'll appreciate it."

The Song was full, and Marty was making a spectacle of herself, much to the amusement of the other butches in the joint and much to the distress of Bobbie. "I hope the bitch passes out," he whispered to a late-arriving Heathcliffe. "I simply *hate* these dirty old dykes!"

Heathcliffe pursed his lips, nodded agreement.

Marty's head was almost level with the bar top. *". . . and all the gay girls, and all the straight men,"* she crooned drunkenly, a song she'd just made up, *"couldn't put Marty together again!"*

Bobbie walked down to Dianne. "Can't you please get her out of here?" he pleaded.

Dianne sneered. "Who the hell wants her? She's a drunken pig. Listen to her crying the blues. Serves the bitch right. Me, I'm splitting. I've had all I can handle, and a hell of a lot more than I can stomach, even for *this* dive!" She tossed a five dollar bill on the bar. "Keep the change, sweetie," she said, sarcasm dripping like acid.

"Marty, Marty, sat on the wall," Marty whimpered. *"Marty, Marty, had a great fall . . ."*

"Will this night *never* end!" Bobbie demanded. "I'm going absolutely out of my mind!"

"I," Heathcliffe added, elegantly, "am getting sick at my stomach. I'll race you to the toilet!"

Dianne left. Marty continued to babble incoherently, making little circles on the bar top with a wet finger. The record on the juke box came to an end, and once again the conversation came up loud.

". . . so I told this fuzz, get lost, buster. Try and take me in. I'll holler rape!"

125

"She's a hell of a good cook, I'll give her that much. But in the sack, forget it. Why, she . . ."

"I get money from home anytime I want it. I just threaten to come back, and the money order's here in twenty-four hours. Another thing . . ."

". . . so forget it. I ain't hustling my tail for you anymore, tiger. Get yourself a new old lady. Oh, sure, go ahead and belt me. Go ahead."

There was a sudden dead silence. Bobbie the bartender sighed. It had to be the police, the vice squad, he thought. That was about the only time the place ever quieted down. He fished for his identification, turned to face the door.

It was Kirk Ward, alone. Kirk walked to a spot beside Marty, and at once a buzz of conversation started up— speculation, rumor.

"Marty?"

She looked at the man hazily. "Mister Bastard," she greeted him, and threw her drink on him.

Kirk took a deep breath. Careful, he told himself. You were expecting something very like this. He brushed the liquor from himself, restraining his temper.

"You'd better come with me. Can you walk?"

She got unsteadily to her feet. "All the gay girls," she intoned solemnly, owlishly, the words blurring together, "and all the straight men, couldn't put . . ." She fell to her knees.

Kirk sighed, bent over and hoisted her to his shoulder. She was surprisingly light.

Dead silence fell over the bar again as he carried her out, in that fashion. At the car, he dumped her into the back seat of the convertible.

He walked around, climbed behind the wheel. Ronnie looked at him with admiration as they pulled away from the curb.

"Kirk, this is wonderful of you."

He waited for the light to change to green, accelerated

smoothly, heading for the freeway and home. "Ron, it's against every instinct. I'm not doing it for her. Not even for you. This is something I had to do for myself. I'll put her back in charge of the firm tomorrow. We'll take her to our home tonight and let her sleep it off in the guest room."

"It isn't her fault," Ronnie said, soberly. "It isn't anyone's fault, I guess."

Kirk turned onto the freeway and accelerated for home. "I guess not," he agreed. "It's the way the world turns. Well, we'll make it, Ronnie."

"Will we, Kirk? Will we really?"

He released a hand from the steering wheel, patted her gently on the thigh. "We'll try, baby. We'll sure as hell try!"

From the back seat came a tuneless wail, barely discernible in the rush of air at the sixty-plus mile per hour speed.

"*. . . and all the gay girls, and all the straight men, couldn't put Marty together again!*"

"We'll try," Ronnie half-whispered. "We'll sure as hell try!"

END